ECHOES OF A PAST

SOPHIE VITESSE

Published by Jeremy Mills Publishing Limited
for Sophie Vitesse

Jeremy Mills Publishing Limited
113 Lidget Street, Lindley, Huddersfield HD3 3JR UK
www.jeremymillspublishing.co.uk

This revised edition published 2010

ISBN 978–1–906600–19–8

For Claire

ACKNOWLEDGEMENTS

MY THANKS TO Gitta Valin, for her enthusiastic support throughout, to Mary Turner, who kindly read the first draft and offered many constructive comments, to Bernard Anscomb, whose encouragement ensured the book was finally completed, and to Reg Valin, many of whose ideas are reflected in the following pages. My special thanks to Simon Walker of Jeremy Mills Publishing for his professionalism and immense attention to detail in bringing this book to publication.

CONTENTS

CHAPTER ONE

AS HE DROVE up the twisting road in the hills above Nice, Peter Barton thought back to the impressions of his first visit to Carros more than twenty-five years earlier. Everything had been completely different from England: not just the scenery and the language but also the abundance of sparkling white buildings and the shimmering blue of the Mediterranean, fast disappearing in his rear view mirror.

During that visit he had stayed with his uncle, his mother's mysterious brother, Pierre, who was rumoured to have business dealings all over the world and who, despite an outward appearance of respectability, somewhat curiously carried a gun in his car.

When asked about his business the response was invariably 'couldn't be better', but little else was ever said that might explain how he came to own a vineyard and such a palatial villa high above the Var river.

Now in his early fifties, Peter was enjoying the freedom that semi-retirement offered following a successful business career. Just over six feet tall, slim, with greying hair and blue eyes, his friends all thought he looked typically English despite being half French.

Reminiscing about Carros, Peter almost collided with a lorry loaded with flowers being driven with characteristic speed by someone in a great hurry to get to the outdoor morning market in the old part of Nice. 'Bloody maniac,' shouted Peter as he swerved perilously close to the edge of the road with its 500-foot drop through the trees and rocks to the valley below.

He was now nearly above the treeline and in the distance could make out the red tiled roof of the villa his uncle had once owned. Set back from the road in spacious grounds, it looked less cared for than how he remembered it, although it still had the air of a property that, if for sale, would attract many would-be purchasers.

He pulled up beside the main gate leading to the house and spoke into an intercom.

'Would it be possible to speak to M. Young?'

An elderly woman answered unintelligibly followed by silence and he was left wondering whether to ring again. A few seconds later he heard the unmistakable voice of Hubert. 'Who is it?'

'It's Peter. I've driven up from Villefranche and, as I mentioned on the phone, I need to talk to you about some queries that have arisen concerning Pierre's estate.'

The gate opened and Peter drove up to the house, noticing that although the lawns were no longer quite so beautifully manicured, flowering shrubs were in abundance and the fountain was as graceful as ever, with its perpetual rainbow created by the sun as it shone through the myriad of tiny droplets.

'Hubert, how good to see you,' said Peter. 'I know from our earlier conversation my visit must be a surprise, but I'll explain after a glass of cold rosé from Pierre's cellar. I had a dreadful hold-up skirting Nice – roadworks on the Corniche – and it's taken over an hour to get here.'

'You look great Peter, although I was concerned to hear that you have encountered some problems with the lawyers. Pierre was never one for administrative details but I assumed they'd all been resolved by now. Why don't you sit on the terrace while I bring out a bottle?'

Peter walked through the floor to ceiling salon windows which opened onto a terrace looking across the lawn to the mountains in the distance. Despite the summer heat there was still some snow on their peaks. 'What an extraordinary contrast,' he thought. 'It's no wonder Pierre enjoyed his life here so much more than in England.'

Hubert appeared with a bottle of wine and also some mineral water. 'I find I can't drink as much as I used to – adding a little mineral water seems to be the answer but I can't say I enjoy it so much. Now, what is it that's brought you here and how can I help?'

'Well, as you know, when uncle Pierre died last year there didn't appear to be a Will until his ex-wife Mary, who you remember he divorced in 1975, turned out some old papers. Amongst them was an exchange of letters with a solicitor which confirmed he had made a Will when he first lived in London not long after the war.'

'Yes, I recall you mentioning it on the phone, but I thought everything had been cleared up once the Will was located.'

'Most of it has,' said Peter. 'But Mary moved into sheltered accommodation recently and, whilst clearing her attic, she found two receipts in an old diary for some unidentified items stored in a village near Salisbury. No address, just a reference to packing cases and Berwick St James. As I believe you first met Pierre in London in the late fifties, I wondered whether they rang a bell with you.'

'Sadly, no. I met him in 1959 when he was running an export and import business just off Oxford Street. I recall he went down to Wiltshire from time to time to meet an American business colleague and often stayed there over the weekend. We used to see a lot of each other in London but, as you know, he moved back to France after the divorce and we lost contact for a while. However, after I sold my business in 1991, he asked me if I would like to join him down here and keep an eye on his vineyard. Initially it was very demanding, but after a lot of hard work we were eventually doing very well, selling our wines not only locally but as far along the coast as Toulon and Marseilles.'

'I must say this is particularly enjoyable,' said Peter. 'May I have another glass?'

'Of course, help yourself. This was an especially good year for the wine but the start of Pierre's problems. As you may be aware, he had always been a bit of a gambler, playing for high stakes at The Clermont when he lived in London. I believe it was one of the many reasons that Mary divorced him. Sadly he never overcame his compulsion, particularly later in life, and spent far too much of his time and money at the casino down in Nice and also in Monte Carlo. He claimed he had a system which occasionally paid off, but when he was in Monte Carlo he used to play on the high stakes tables that the Russians frequent and his losses really started to escalate.'

'Is that what led him to sell you the villa and the vineyard.'

'In the end it was inevitable. We had a disaster with the crop after a poor summer, and much more rain than expected. We had just negotiated a very large order with a supermarket group but were unable to fulfil it as production was only 60% of our expectations. They cancelled the order and we were then forced to sell most of our production cheaply, much of it to the hotels and bars he used to frequent in Nice and Cannes. He'd also been speculating on the gold price – he took one or two largish positions which turned out to be poor calls.'

'But surely it couldn't have been that bad.'

'I'm afraid it was. He'd been borrowing heavily, with the vineyard as security, and the bank finally decided that enough was enough. It was agreed I would buy the house and the vineyard at a pretty generous price. I guess it was partly to reflect the contribution I'd made in building up the value of the business and also because he couldn't bear to feel he'd have to leave here if it went to someone else. As you know, he stayed on at the lodge but after everything that had happened, his health deteriorated quite quickly, he became very forgetful and he died shortly afterwards. But Peter, why are you so concerned about the packing cases you mention – surely the lawyers dealt with everything once the Will was finally located?'

'It was, more or less, but I gather there are still some loose ends,' said Peter. 'You probably remember the fuss his mistress, Mme Martin, made when she claimed she knew about other assets he had hinted at. Well, apparently she hired a private detective who has been asking a lot of questions and her daughter, Suzanne, called me in London last week to say she'd heard that Maître Simon, the lawyer who is handling the winding up of the estate, is anxious to establish if there is anything else of value that has not been accounted for. Seemingly, he is concerned about potential inheritance tax implications. I was told something similar when I spoke to the lawyers in England so I've have promised to meet her in Nice before I fly back to London.'

'Do you have any idea what they're looking for?'

'No, that's why I came up here to see you – I thought Pierre might have mentioned Berwick St James to you at some stage in the past, or you might know of a connection with it, since the two of you were so close.'

'I really can't help but I'll call a couple of his old acquaintances just in case they have any ideas. If I get any useful information, I'll ring you at the hotel.'

Back in Villefranche, Peter sat on his hotel balcony looking at the yachts bobbing gently in the bay as the sun, a fiery red orb, disappeared behind the headland. It was easy to understand why his uncle loved this part of France so much and had chosen to live here for most of his life, even though he was born in the north and spent his early years there. Had things been different, Peter could imagine living here himself or at the very least having an apartment in Nice or somewhere along the coast. The perfect bolt-hole – sun, sea and for much of the year even skiing, if one were prepared for a two-hour drive into the mountains.

His reverie was interrupted by the phone.

'Hello Peter, it's Suzanne, I was just talking to Hubert, who told me you are already here. How long are you staying?'

'A couple more days – news certainly travels fast!'

'Any chance of getting together tomorrow?'

'Of course, when would be best for you?'

'How about lunch in Nice?'

'That's fine – would the terrace of the Westminster suit you at 12.30?'

'Great, I'll see you then.'

Peter replaced the phone, still wondering why Suzanne was so keen to see him. He had met her two or three times before and had always enjoyed her company. A bright, stylish and sophisticated real estate agent, she handled sales and lettings of luxurious properties in Cap Ferrat and Beaulieu, and had a reputation for being a highly effective operator. The lunch should be fun even though he was still intrigued by the reason for the call.

The next morning, Peter drove into Nice and left the hire car in a car park on the Promenade des Anglais. He popped into the Barclays branch a couple of blocks away to pick up some cash and was surprised by the conversion rate of the pound to the euro. 'No wonder everything seems to cost so much more nowadays,' he thought. 'Sterling has lost more than 5% of its value since I was here last year!'

He arrived at the Westminster, found a shady table on the terrace, ordered a beer and watched the passers-by. Most were female, almost all surprisingly well dressed and many with small dogs. 'What is it with people in Nice and their dogs?' he mused.

'Hello Peter, how lovely to see you.' He turned on hearing a familiar French voice with the slightest mid-Atlantic accent. Suzanne was staring down from behind huge dark glasses, her hair swept back from her face and wearing a black silk dress with a slim cream belt which complemented her designer shoes. Tanned legs completed the outfit.

Peter kissed her and immediately tried to recall the name of the perfume she habitually wore. It suited her perfectly, fresh but with a subtle fragrance he remembered finding rather alluring when last they met.

'And it's especially good to see you Suzanne – let me get you a drink.'

A waiter appeared. 'I'd like a glass of Chablis,' said Suzanne.

'Shall we take a look at the menu, before it gets too busy,' said Peter.

'I recommend the salade niçoise – it's one of their specialities.'

'Good idea,' said Peter. 'I'll order them for both of us.'

'Hubert tells me you were asking him if he knew anything about some boxes that Pierre is supposed to have tucked away somewhere in England. Maman believes they might contain something of value and she has been digging into his past to try to find out more about them. As I mentioned, the lawyer in Nice, Maître Simon, has been pressing her for information in case there is anything else which might affect their final submission to the tax authorities. Since you also seem to be interested in the mysterious boxes, I thought we might compare notes.'

'I don't know much myself,' said Peter. 'The lawyers who have been tying things up in London raised this with me recently, as I am the main beneficiary. I guess it has arisen as a result of discussions with Maître Simon and also their own enquiries. I suspect that whatever is in the packing cases, wherever they are, may go back to the time not long after the war when Pierre was involved in business dealings with some Americans he met in North Africa.'

'What makes you think that?'

'Simply because they were also an acquaintance of a shady Croatian called Goran Dantic for whom Pierre had arranged some introductions in London. Apparently one of the Americans settled in England after the war and bought a small pied-à-terre in Kensington Church Street. Not long afterwards he got married and bought a house in Somerset at a place called Milborne Port where Pierre used to stay occasionally.'

'How do you know all this?'

'Partially from his ex-wife Mary and also from the lawyers in London.'

'So you think this may be the place where the boxes are stored?'

'It seems possible. I gather Pierre rarely ventured out of London. Berwick St James is a small place only about twelve miles from Milborne Port – it wouldn't have taken him more than twenty minutes to get there if he wanted to tuck some things away for safety.'

'That's interesting,' said Suzanne. 'Because Maman was convinced he had stored some items of value before he left England and always intended to retrieve them – but I don't understand why they're still there.'

'Nor do I,' said Peter. 'But this has to be cleared up before the lawyers can sign off.'

'What are you proposing to do next?'

'I'm not sure, but for a start I'd be interested to get some idea how Pierre managed to lose so much money in Monte Carlo a few years ago. Do you fancy a trip to the casino this evening?'

'That would be fun. Incidentally, what did you think of the salade niçoise?'

'It was fine, although the tuna seemed more fishy than Pierre's business activities!'

Back at the hotel, Peter picked up a message to ring the lawyers in London. After finishing the call, he rang Hubert.

'Hubert, it was good to see you yesterday and thanks for sparing the time. I've just been talking to the lawyers in London about one or two matters – is there any chance of seeing you again tomorrow before I leave?'

'Certainly, but was your meeting with Suzanne useful?'

'Not really. I think she was probably trying to find out whether I knew anything more than her mother.'

'Helene Martin is really stirring things up and seems to be preventing Maître Simon from finalising things. It's typical of the way she behaved with Pierre. Once the relationship became fairly permanent, she really got him under her thumb. She even tried to get involved with the running of the vineyard when we had all those problems a few years ago. I also suspect she encouraged his gambling as she liked to be seen at the tables in Monte Carlo and never seemed very concerned by his losses.'

'I find that very curious. When would be a good time for us to meet – I'm flying back at 5.20?'

'How about an early lunch at the Hotel du Cap,' said Hubert. 'Say around 12.15?'

'What a civilised thought, I'll see you there tomorrow.'

Peter decided the pool looked enticing and, finding a quiet corner under a shade, he pondered on the significance of Hubert's comments. It seemed fairly clear that Mme Martin had not discouraged Pierre from his extravagant lifestyle, which was a little surprising in the light of the financial problems she must have known about and had led to the sale of the vineyard. Had she in some way connived with Hubert to increase Pierre's financial problems and thus precipitate a cut price sale or had she thought his financial situation was much better than was now apparent? Either way, it was easy to understand why she was interested in trying to find out more about the mysterious boxes hidden somewhere in England.

He decided to take a quick dip before going up to his room to get ready for the trip to Monte Carlo.

At eight o'clock, Suzanne called up from reception. 'I'm down below with a taxi – do you want to drive or shall I ask him to wait?'

'Parking is never easy in Monte Carlo. Going by taxi would be ideal if he doesn't have another booking. I'll be with you in a couple of minutes.'

Before going down Peter put his debit card in the safe. 'Just a precaution,' he thought to himself. 'I don't want to get tempted into high stakes betting if I'm losing.'

'Hello Suzanne, I hope you're feeling lucky.'

'I'm not much of a gambler but a friend of mine swears by a split on 33/36 and claims that one should never leave twenty-one uncovered! I tend to be much less adventurous but might wager a few euros either on High or Low or else Red or Black.'

'Probably very wise, I suspect that Pierre lost most of his money following a so-called system that was doomed to failure.'

'I think you're right. Maman said that he had a favourite combination of numbers but he was so superstitious that he was only happy to bet on them if zero had come up twice within a dozen spins.'

'Shall we have a drink at the Hôtel de Paris before we try our luck?' said Peter.

'That would be fun and also a good opportunity to study some of Monaco's seriously rich tax exiles who invariably seem to be there at this time of the day.'

The taxi pulled up outside the hotel, in front of a line of Maybachs, Ferraris and a solitary Bugatti that was catching the eye of many passers-by. Porsches and Aston Martins were also in evidence but apparently not considered to be quite in the same league, as they were tucked a little further back.

They found a table in the bar and ordered champagne cocktails.

'I can readily understand what attracted Pierre to this place,' Peter said, eying the room. 'It must be nearly ten years since I was last here but it never seems to change or lose its special fascination.'

'I suspect its attraction is that it still has the aura of an old style "grand hotel" in an era when the emphasis is now so much on change. Nowadays many of the long established hotels seem to be undertaking major refurbishment and modernisation programmes that often totally extinguish their original style and personality. Hotels like this concentrate on maintaining an old-fashioned air of discreet and exemplary service which is still very popular with discerning visitors.'

'Well it seems to be very successful judging by the clientele. Are you ready to chance your luck?'

'Why not,' said Suzanne. 'I'm only planning to have a couple of bets on even chances – unless of course I'm extremely lucky!'

They crossed the square to the casino, whose grand entrance was more appropriate to a major art gallery or museum. Inside, the ornate architecture would have done justice to a palace and the lofty moulded ceiling only emphasised the curious contrast with the pygmy-like gaming tables which were dotted within the various rooms. At the tables voices were hushed and almost reverential as croupiers either spun roulette wheels or dealt cards. Around each table were individual players and behind them groups of curious spectators, many of them tourists anxious to enjoy yet another new experience on their itineraries, but seemingly reluctant to participate.

'I'm going to look at the play on one of the higher stakes roulette tables,' said Peter.

'Are you all right here?'

'Yes, go ahead. I'll probably lose immediately, in which case I'll come and find you.'

Peter wandered past tables where optimistic players were hoping that luck would be favouring them. Some were very cautious making one small bet on the even chances, others had a certain bravado in their approach and appeared to be quite reckless in the scale and amounts of their wagering, scattering chips on individual numbers in the hope of winning at odds of thirty-five to one.

He went into a slightly smaller room, where two roulette tables were surrounded by a cross section of players, mostly of Chinese and Middle Eastern origin. He also noticed one or two Russians who were betting as much as one thousand euros on single numbers. He estimated that for every spin of the wheel well over one hundred thousand euros were being wagered. One or two players seemed to be having some success, but the majority were steadily losing. Here the atmosphere was much more clinical; none of them, winners or losers, registered noticeable emotion, whatever the outcome of each spin.

'I really can't understand how they can lose such large sums without being affected,' thought Peter. 'I wonder where their money comes from.'

After watching a few more spins, enlivened by the appearance of Zero, which briefly elicited a murmur of response from the players, he returned to the main room to find Suzanne.

'Any luck?'

'I'm twenty euros up after half a dozen bets. I think I might quit while I'm ahead.'

'Good idea, do you mind watching whilst I have a flutter?'

'Not at all. What was it like in the inner sanctum?'

'Very strange. As far as I could tell nobody got much pleasure from winning, nor did they seem to be particularly fazed by losing. I saw one player lose 20,000 euros two spins running – it certainly helped me to understand how Pierre could have lost so much money but I still don't understand why.'

Peter asked the croupier for 250 euros' worth of chips and played for about half an hour, placing split bets of two numbers and corners of four. He had varying fortune, fluctuating between a profit of eighty euros and losses of over one hundred. After a couple of good wins on rouge, he decided to quit whilst he was ahead and he picked up 420 euros when he cashed in.

'It's great that we both won,' said Peter. 'Although it's only a small amount, it'll cover the cost of the taxi and our drinks. It's always good to have a free evening!'

They picked up a cab outside the casino and were soon back at Peter's hotel.

'I'm going back to London later tomorrow afternoon. It's been great fun catching up with you – can I give you a call when next I'm here, probably early next month?'

'I've enjoyed the evening enormously, Peter, and it was good to see you again. I do hope you manage to sort things out when you get back but, in the meantime, I'll look forward to seeing you again soon.'

She kissed him lightly on the lips before getting back into the taxi. As he walked back to his room the fragrance of her perfume stayed with him – but this time for very much longer.

CHAPTER TWO

THE NEXT MORNING Peter called Richard Anstruther, the lawyer in London.

'When did Pierre liquidate his remaining assets in Britain?'

'The small mews house in Holland Park and the pictures went in 1995 and I believe the DB6 was bought by an ex-business colleague at about the same time.'

'Do you know how much he raised and anything about who bought the car?'

'I can't remember exactly – perhaps around £800,000. I'll have a look in the files to see if there's any information about the car buyer.'

'That would be very helpful – it would also be useful to know who witnessed the sale documents. I'll be back in London tomorrow and will be in touch.'

As Peter had time to kill before meeting Hubert for lunch, he decided to pay a quick visit to the Ephrussi Villa and Garden overlooking Villefranche and Beaulieu, which were on his route to lunch. He wandered through the villa with its wonderful collection of sculptures, porcelain and paintings and then sat for a while in the exquisite garden amidst fountains, ornamental patios, shaded paths, lily ponds and a mass of flowering shrubs.

'When next I'm in Nice I must come here with Suzanne, it's absolutely magical,' he thought. 'But in the meantime, I'd better not be late for lunch.'

When he arrived at the Hotel du Cap Hubert was waiting under the pine trees on the Terrace.

'I've ordered a bottle of Sauvignon – is that OK for you?'

'Perfect,' said Peter. 'Thanks for sparing the time to meet up again.'

'It's no hardship – this is one of my favourite places for lunch, being so cool and shady. How was your visit to the casino?'

'A small profit and very entertaining, but I can't understand why Pierre went there so often.'

'Oh, I can understand it, I've often had a flutter myself. The problem for Pierre was that I suspect it was a bit of an addiction and, as I mentioned, Helene was always keen to accompany him. Regrettably the debts he incurred, coupled with the problems at the vineyard, precipitated his downfall.'

'Why on earth didn't she discourage his gambling habit.'

'I can't imagine – maybe you should ask her yourself, Peter.'

'I probably will, next time I'm here. However, in the meantime, I wanted to see if you could remember the names of any of Pierre's friends or business colleagues at the time you first met in London. I know from Mary he had dealings with someone living in Kensington who also had a house in Somerset – can you recall anything about him?'

'I think you're talking about an American who was friendly with Goran Dantic, a Croatian contact of Pierre's, who I also knew slightly. Goran was a rather odd character who had a reputation for "liberating" post-war assets in eastern Europe. I think Pierre may have first met the American in North Africa in the war. If it wasn't there it was at a party when Goran was trying to get some financial backing for one of his slightly dodgy projects. I believe the American was looking for products to import to the USA and, amongst other activities, Pierre represented a large biscuit manufacturer in Holland. I seem to recall that Pierre helped him to become their selling agent in America.'

'That more or less ties in with what Mary told me, although she thought they'd met in North Africa.'

'More than possible, Pierre often disappeared to Marrakech on business trips and honeymooned there when he and Mary married in 1945.'

'You can't remember the American's name or anything more about him?'

'It's such a long time ago but Mary might have an address or phone number.'

'I rather doubt it – as I mentioned yesterday, she had a major clear-out when she moved.'

'Wait a minute,' said Hubert. 'When Pierre came back to France he sold his London business to Goran's son. It might be worth contacting him to see if he can help.'

'Do you have any idea where I could find him?'

'Let me check when I get back to the villa. In the meantime shall we order – if you like shellfish, the langoustines are delicious!'

'Sounds an excellent choice to me, and maybe some of their local cheese to follow.'

After lunch Peter went back to his hotel, picked up his bags and checked out. At the airport, he went to the passenger lounge and made a call to Hubert.

'Any joy with that phone number?'

'Yes, I have a number but I don't know whether you'll still find him there. His name is Branko Dantic and the number I have is where Pierre was last in contact with him.'

Peter took the number down before a quick visit to duty-free, which offered little of interest apart from the cheese he had enjoyed so much at lunch. He decided to buy a portion as a memento and hoped it would travel well.

For once the flight left on time and, after an exchange of pleasantries with the passenger in the adjoining seat, Peter picked up the earphones to listen to some music. His thoughts wandered over his discussions with Hubert and Suzanne, neither of which had been as informative as he had hoped. He found it difficult to understand how Helene Martin could have allowed Pierre to continue to gamble so frequently and recklessly without trying to stop him unless she might have been conspiring with Hubert to add to his financial pressures and force the sale of the villa and vineyard at a substantially lower price than their market value. Hubert had seemed evasive when Peter talked about Helene Martin's behaviour, which added to his misgivings. While meeting Suzanne had been fun, he somehow had the feeling she had been trying to pump him for information. He assumed this was probably on behalf of her mother, whom Peter had never much cared for and who was quite obviously motivated by the hope of financial gain, despite the suggestion that her desire to find out more about the lost packing cases was to help Maître Simon to close his files. In addition to gaining a better understanding of the way his uncle had managed to get himself into such a financial mess, Peter felt that something else positive might be achieved from his visit if he could contact Branko Dantic. If that proved to be a dead end, his only hope was that Richard Anstruther might be able to turn up something useful about the buyer of his uncle's DB6.

When he got back to his flat, just off the King's Road, there were a couple of messages waiting for him: one from Pierre's ex-wife Mary, asking him to call her once he was back in London, the other from Suzanne, saying how much she had enjoyed seeing him again and hoping they could keep in touch. 'Probably inspired by her mother,' thought Peter cynically, although he was nonetheless pleased she had called. As it was late, he decided against calling Mary until the following morning.

Peter awoke to grey skies. 'What a contrast to the south of France,' he thought. 'But London has so many other saving graces.'

After a shower, a croissant and coffee and a quick look through the accumulated mail he called Mary.

'Just back from the south of France and I picked up your message.'

'I thought I'd call to see whether the trip had been useful as I know you were hoping it would help to bring matters to a conclusion. I'm beginning to wish I hadn't turned up those wretched pieces of paper in Pierre's diary – they seem to have been more of a nuisance than a help.'

'Well I saw Hubert and I found out more about Pierre's business problems and also his gambling habit. I also met up with Suzanne, who is Helene Martin's daughter,' said Peter.

'I can't say I totally trusted Hubert. He spent a lot of time with Goran Dantic, who I thought was a very dubious character and first got Pierre into gambling in the West End. I'm pretty sure Hubert also arranged the sale of Pierre's business in London to Goran's son Branko and contrived to get a commission from both parties!'

'Really?' said Peter. 'He said nothing to me about that when we talked and only mentioned Branko when I pressed him about contacts from Pierre's past.'

'Did you know, Pierre sold the villa and the vineyard to Hubert very cheaply? I found it difficult to believe the price when I heard – more than 10% below the market value. Pierre must have been under considerable financial pressure to have agreed such a price.'

'That's extraordinary, Hubert gave me the impression Pierre had asked him to buy the property, almost as a favour.'

'No, I think it was quite the opposite. Hubert pushed him into the sale – allegedly to save the business.'

'How very curious,' said Peter. 'Hubert is proving to be quite an intriguing character.'

'Let me know if there is anything more I can do to help, although my memory isn't as good as it used to be. Do pop down see me some time – it would be such a treat to see you.'

'Of course I will – have you settled in to your new flat?'

'More or less, but I seem to be surrounded by old people!'

'Mary, you're incorrigible,' said Peter. 'You take good care of yourself.'

'Well, I don't suppose anyone else will.'

'You never change – I'll see you soon.'

Mary's comments about Hubert made Peter feel that in future he would have to be very careful about what he told him. It seemed he might not be entirely trustworthy and could even be hiding information that would help to clarify some of Pierre's past activities.

He called the number Hubert had given him. There was no response but the voice on the answerphone said 'this is Branko, please leave a message'.

Peter decided it would be easier to call back later rather than attempting a complicated explanation and called Richard Anstruther.

'Have you been able to turn up anything of interest from the files in connection with the sale of Pierre's UK assets?'

'Yes, I rather think it would be worth a meeting – could you make 11.30 this morning?'

'I'll see you then.'

Peter arrived at the office in Old Burlington Street just after 11.15. He was shown into the reception area and whilst he was waiting browsed through a couple of the firm's brochures. 'Remarkable how many services law firms now offer,' thought Peter. 'And judging by the decor they must be flourishing. But who ever heard of a struggling legal practice!'

He was shown into a meeting room by a secretary who enquired whether he would like coffee, tea or herbal tea.

'Coffee would be fine,' said Peter.

'Mr Anstruther won't be more than a couple of minutes.'

Peter looked at the art on the walls and concluded that 'flourishing' was a bit of an understatement. Three original paintings by well regarded modern artists flanked an extremely expensive piece of sculpture.

Richard Anstruther was as good as his secretary's word and appeared almost immediately. 'I hope I haven't kept you, I had to finish a call.'

'Not at all, just admiring your collection.'

'They are rather fine, aren't they? One of my colleagues is a bit of an aficionado and has done rather well for us. It's become a very important component of the partners' pension fund.'

'Judging by some of these, imminent retirement must be a serious option!'

'Now, now Peter we work very hard and we give our clients an excellent service – I think you're going to be quite pleased with our efforts when I tell you what we've been able to find out.'

'I'm all ears.'

'When we spoke a couple of days ago you asked me about the sale of Pierre's car. I had a look through the file and in view of the diary Mary unearthed in the attic I was particularly interested in the purchaser of two of his pictures.'

'What was so interesting about them?'

'Their address was in Berwick St James.'

'You're not serious,' said Peter.

'I certainly am and, more to the point, I checked with directory enquiries and the purchaser is still at that address.'

'Richard, surely that's more than just a coincidence – there must be some sort of connection between the buyer and whatever is stored in the packing cases there.'

'I'd be rather inclined to that view, but I imagine you'll want to pay a visit to check it out for yourself.'

'Absolutely – you really have excelled yourselves. Is there anything else of interest in the file?'

'Nothing that appears too relevant other than this – I hope it proves to be a fruitful lead,' said Richard.

'If it helps to resolve this mystery, I suspect that when I receive your fee invoice, I won't mind feeling I'm making a sizeable personal contribution towards your next work of art!'

'Peter, it pains me to think what you are inferring – let me get my secretary to give you the purchaser's details.'

As he left the office, Peter felt that at last he was getting closer to locating the mysterious boxes and, more important, what they might contain. When he was back to his flat he looked at the information on the paper that Richard's secretary had given him – Mike Docherty, The Old Vicarage, Berwick St James – followed by a phone number.

He thought for a while and decided to phone right away.

A woman's voice answered, 'Nicola Docherty'.

'Hello,' said Peter. 'Could I speak to Mike Docherty?'

'Who's calling?'

'My name is Peter Barton. He doesn't know me but I wanted to have a word with him about a couple of paintings he bought at auction some years ago from my uncle.'

'Would you mind holding a moment?'

Peter waited with growing excitement until a softly spoken voice with a slight American accent came on the line.

'This is Mike Docherty, how can I help you?'

'It's rather a long story but I'm calling because I believe you bought a couple of paintings at an auction that used to belong to my uncle, Pierre Vaillant.'

'Why yes, he was a close friend of my dad and I often admired the pictures when he and I visited your uncle in his mews house in London. When he arranged for the sale of the house and contents a few years ago I bought the pictures. He also had an Aston Martin which I'd have liked, but my wife, Nicola, wasn't very enthusiastic. But why are you calling? They're not forgeries, I hope.'

'Not as far as I know,' said Peter, 'but I needed to know that you were the person who bought them and I wanted to ask if you might know anything at all about some boxes or packing cases that my uncle might have stored in Berwick St James many years ago.'

'What sort of packing cases?' said Mike.

'I simply don't know,' said Peter, and then explained the circumstances that had led him to make the call.

'Well, we have a number of outhouses that were used as stabling and for storing hay when my dad was alive. He used to ride when he was a boy in Montana and continued over here well into his sixties, until he had a fall. We've always intended to tidy them up and even considered turning them into holiday cottages but never got round to it. There are a lot of old tools and other clutter, as this was also a farm before my dad bought it. I think there may be a few packing cases buried under the rest of the rubbish but I've never looked in them since we inherited the place.'

'Would you mind if I came down to take a look?'

'Any time – I'll try to clear up a bit so you can get at them.'

'Would it be convenient if I drove down Saturday morning? I'd be with you around half past ten.'

'That's OK with me.'

'Thanks Mike – see you then.'

Peter found it difficult to control the excitement he felt following his conversation with Mike Docherty. Finding his uncle's boxes had seemed an impossibility, now it appeared that they had at last been located. 'Don't count your chickens,' thought Peter. 'Just because there are some packing cases in a building in Berwick St James doesn't necessarily mean that they're the ones you've been trying to find. Even so it does seem an extraordinary coincidence.'

He decided to try calling Branko Dantic – this time successfully.

'Hello, my name is Peter Barton, I'm Pierre Vaillant's nephew. Sadly my uncle died last year in Nice and I'm trying to help his lawyers to tie up some loose ends relating to his estate. Am I right in thinking that you acquired his business interests in London when he left England?'

'Yes, that was way back in the seventies, why do you ask?'

'I'm trying to sort out a few loose ends in connection with his estate and Hubert Young, his old business partner, gave me your number. Could you spare the time for us to get together today for half an hour?'

'I don't know if I can help but I could meet you later this afternoon – say about four o'clock at the Carlton Tower?'

'That would be ideal for me. How will I recognise you?'

'I'm just over six feet tall, in my mid fifties, long brown hair and will be wearing a blue suit. How about you?'

'Similar age and height, greyish hair. I'll reserve a table in my name.'

Peter arrived at the Carlton Tower at a quarter to four, sat at a table opposite the entrance and ordered tea. Just before four o'clock, he spotted someone who looked like Branko and he waved him over.

'Peter Barton, I'm very pleased to see you and thanks for sparing the time.'

Branko's description was fairly accurate, although his tailor was clearly adept at disguising a burgeoning waistline that had not been mentioned. He also had the sort of tan that looked as though it didn't come from a bottle.

'Hello Peter – it's good to meet you at last. Your uncle often spoke of you as his "English" nephew.'

'Yes, well, as you probably know, my dad was English and married Pierre's much younger sister when she and Pierre were living in England. My parents both died some years ago and as a result I rather lost touch with him over the last few years.'

'You mentioned some loose ends relating to his estate.'

'Yes, I'm trying to find out a little more about Pierre's activities before he moved back to France and also to locate some of his possessions that may be stored in a place called Berwick St James.'

'That place rings a bell with me – I seem to recall that's where an American acquaintance of Pierre's lived.'

'Was his name Docherty?'

'Yes, that's it, Ted Docherty. He was a close friend of another American, called Mark Carter, who was in business with Pierre after the war. Carter married an English girl and I think he bought a property somewhere near Salisbury, as he liked that part of southern England, having been based there with an American bomber squadron. I seem to recall he and Docherty flew together on a number of missions and both decided they would settle in this country when the war ended.'

'Was that a place called Milborne Port?' said Peter.

'That's the place – I know Pierre used to go down there quite often to stay the weekend as my father also went with him sometimes. I think Pierre may have got to know them during the war when he was involved in liaison work between the Free French in London and resistance movements in France.'

'Have you any idea whether Carter lives there any longer?'

'No, but I have his address and phone number at home and it would be easy for me to check.'

'I'd be very grateful if you could.'

'So without being too nosy, what is it you are trying to find out?'

'I'm not sure but I spoke to Mike Docherty, Ted's son, who thinks there may be some packing cases stored in an outhouse at this place Berwick St James. Once I've had a look inside them, I may have a better idea whether they contain anything of value.'

'Well, from what I gathered whenever my dad talked about the war those guys had some interesting experiences together, so I can imagine the contents could produce a few surprises.'

'That's what I believe,' said Peter. 'Pierre's mistress in France certainly thinks so.'

'Is that someone called Helene Martin?'

'Yes, why do you ask?'

'Simply because I had a call from a private detective on her behalf a few weeks ago asking me if I had any old papers or personal effects of Pierre's.'

'She's certainly making a lot of effort to try to locate whatever Pierre left in those boxes. What did you say to him?'

'I asked if he could be more specific as I have a lot of papers relating to Pierre's business dealings prior to him selling me the company. I had the impression the guy didn't have much idea what he was after, and he didn't make any reference to Berwick St James.'

'If he contacts you again would you mind keeping our conversation to yourself?' said Peter. 'And would you let me know?'

'Sure, and in the meantime I'll check whether Mark Carter still lives at Milborne Port.'

'That'd be great – thanks so much for your help.'

'Not at all – if you find anything of interest will you let me know? I was a great fan of your uncle and he was very kind to me when I was younger and still living here. If you see Hubert again soon give him my best.'

Back at his flat, Peter poured himself a large whisky and pondered the day's events. It seemed clear that the connection between his uncle, Ted Docherty and Mark Carter was somehow associated with what Pierre had been doing in the war when he had been with the Free French in London and giving support to the French Resistance. It also seemed apparent that if there were packing cases in Berwick St James they must be the ones he was seeking, but he wondered why they were still there and, if they were so important, why Pierre hadn't transferred the contents to France long ago.

The phone rang. It was Branko again.

'I just checked on Mark Carter. He wasn't there, but a housekeeper said he was out fishing and would be back later. I didn't leave any message. Would you like to make a note of the number?'

'Please,' said Peter as he jotted it down. 'Many thanks – I'll keep you posted.'

CHAPTER THREE

ON SATURDAY MORNING, Peter left his flat just before nine o'clock. Traffic out of London was reasonably light and he was soon on the M3. It was a beautiful sunny day, and as he drove along the undulating sections of the A303, he felt at times as though he was flying. Passing the RAF station at Boscombe Down, he breasted a hill and was presented with a bird's-eye view of Stonehenge, starkly magnificent in its splendid isolation. A few minutes later he drew up outside the Old Vicarage in Berwick St James. He was a few minutes early and sat in the car feeling a little apprehensive about what he might be about to find, if the packing cases to which Mike Docherty had referred did belong to Pierre.

'Better get on with it,' he said to himself and rang the door bell.

The door was opened by a smiling, middle-aged man dressed in a denim shirt and a tired-looking pair of cord trousers. Fair hair peered from beneath a cap which appeared to have had an encounter with some cobwebs.

'Hello, you must be Peter. Sorry about my appearance but I've been trying to clear up a bit so you can get to those packing cases. Did you have any problem finding us?'

'Not at all, the drive was very straightforward.'

'Do you want to take a look right away or would you like a cup of coffee?'

'That would be great,' said Peter as they walked through to the kitchen.

Whilst Mike made the coffee, Peter looked around the kitchen. An Aga range dominated one wall and a solid oak dresser provided ample space for an eclectic mixture of china, vases, herb racks and glasses as well as a huge bowl of fruit. The centre of the room was dominated by a massive oak trestle table to which Mike brought two mugs of coffee and a plate of biscuits.

'Make yourself comfortable,' said Mike, 'and have one of these biscuits which my wife makes, I think you'll enjoy them.'

Peter tried a shortcake which was embedded with small chunks of chocolate and nuts.

'They're absolutely delicious – has she ever considered baking them for your local shops?'

'Funnily enough, she does produce a few for local restaurants and the Acorn Inn, which you probably saw as you drove through the village, but mostly they're just for friends and as Christmas presents.'

'Well maybe once we get to know each other better, she'd consider adding me to the list!'

'I'm sure she'll be delighted to know she has yet another fan – shall I show you where you can find the packing cases and then I'll leave you to it?'

They walked down a path through what appeared to be a large kitchen garden, past two greenhouses and into a stable area with loose boxes and other outbuildings. Mike pointed to one of them. 'They're in the right hand corner at the back under some sheeting. It's very dusty but you should be able to get to them without any difficulty.'

Peter pushed open the battered wooden door of a building full of benches, chairs, tables, garden equipment and tools and what appeared to be small items of agricultural machinery. His eyes gradually grew accustomed to the gloom and he saw the sheeting to which Mike had referred. Covered in a thick layer of dust he could just make out the initials 'PLV' on the front of what appeared to be a couple of packing cases.

With a combination of excitement and apprehension, he pulled away the sheeting and dragged them closer to the entrance. Using a chisel he prised open the lid of the first case. Inside, under what looked like an old table cloth, were two or three small boxes and some files tied up with cord. He flicked through the files, the contents of which were in French, and beyond his limited familiarity with the language. He then turned his attention to the other case, which contained a number of faded photographs in frames each wrapped in a cloth, a couple more files, a revolver and two medals with fraying ribbons. The rest of the contents appeared to be of no significance – a few books by French authors, a pair of tarnished silver candlesticks, an old leather briefcase and a set of keys. Finally he opened one of the small boxes which contained some letters written in French and also a number of postcards from what looked like holiday resorts.

After a while, and having checked his watch, he realised it was nearly lunchtime. Since the light was so poor inside the building that it was almost impossible to read, he thought the wisest thing would be to leave further inspection of the files and letters until he got back to London and he decided to pack everything in a couple of holdalls he had left in the car. As he crossed the yard, Mike called out from one of the other buildings.

'Anything of interest? I hope they were the boxes you were looking for.'

'Yes, they were Pierre's, but they consisted almost entirely of papers and letters. I haven't gone through everything but there doesn't seem to be anything of value, and it's too dark and my French isn't good enough to make sense of what's in the files.'

'What are you going to do with them now?'

'I think the best thing is to take them back with me and I can then get the lawyers to go through the files and see if there's anything of significance in them.'

'Do you need a hand?'

'That's very kind. There's nothing particularly heavy. I'm just getting a couple of holdalls from the car to put them in and then I'll be off.'

When Peter had finished he went back to the house.

'Mike, you've been very kind. Once I've gone through everything I'll give you a call and let you know what I've found. However, in the meantime, what do I owe you in storage for what must be well over twenty-five years?'

'It's a pleasure – as you can see, we didn't need the building for anything so we're happy to be getting rid of a bit more clutter. Maybe it'll provide the impetus to get shot of the rest of the rubbish and encourage us to get cracking with our plans to refurbish some of the buildings.'

'Just before I go, I wanted to ask if you ever had contact with an old American friend of your father's called Mark Carter. I believe they served together in bomber squadrons during the war and they were also good friends of Pierre's'.

'Sure, I don't know him particularly well but Dad used to meet up with him and Pierre quite frequently some years ago. Dad died not long after Pierre went back to France so, apart from exchanging the occasional Christmas card, we've not had much contact for quite a while. Why, did you want to get in touch?'

'Maybe, perhaps I could let you know.'

Peter stopped off at a country pub on the way back to London and sat in the garden with a ploughman's lunch and a glass of local bitter. He could imagine how attractive such pubs could have been to US airmen like Carter and Docherty after returning from yet another lengthy sortie, when they wanted to unwind and put the hazards of a bombing raid behind them. Was it even possible that the two of them and Pierre had spent time together sitting out in this garden all those years ago?

When he got back to London, Peter went carefully through the contents of the holdalls and put all of the files and their contents together to take to his lawyer. He tried to clean up the photographs, which were very faded, but in a couple he could just distinguish two young airmen in US uniforms alongside a civilian who looked very much like Pierre. On the back of one was scrawled 'France, 1944' and on another 'New Year's Day 1945'. One of the others showed what again looked like Pierre with an attractive, dark haired young woman who had her arm through his and was looking up at him with what was evidently considerable affection. There were two or three others of the same young woman who obviously enjoyed posing for whoever was taking the photograph. On the back of one of these was the caption 'Delphine, July 1944'. There were also photographs of the same young woman with a baby and another of her with a small girl.

Peter now turned his attention to the boxes and the handwritten letters and postcards they contained. All were in French and mostly in the same handwriting. A combination of virtually unreadable writing and his limited French meant that he could barely decipher any of them.

Peter noticed with increasing surprise that many of them opened with the words 'Mon Cher Pierre' and were signed with increasing evidence of affection by the name 'Delphine'.

Finally he opened an envelope that contained the postcards, most of which were simple greetings from Delphine, then suddenly Peter was confronted by five cards tied with white cotton in what was unmistakeably a child's writing, all addressed to 'Cher Oncle Pierre'.

Peter stared at the cards in astonishment and turned them over and over in his hands. They were all from different places in France – most of which appeared to be holiday resorts – and were dated between 1950 and 1959. Still in disbelief, he tried to make sense of what he had discovered. It was clear that his uncle had somehow been involved in a relationship with a young French woman in France just before the end of the war and, from what he could see of the postmarks, this had continued for many years after it had ended. But who was the mysterious child and why was she addressing Pierre as 'Oncle'?

He realised that the only way to get an answer to these questions was to have the contents of the files and the letters from Delphine translated as soon as possible. He decided he would call Richard Anstruther to see if he could help.

'Richard, it's Peter. Sorry to bother you on the weekend but I followed up the contact you gave me the other day and went down to Berwick St James to meet up with Mike Docherty. I found a couple of packing cases containing files which are rather too sophisticated for my schoolboy French. There are also some letters of a personal nature from a French woman called Delphine. Is there someone you could recommend who is discreet and might be able translate them for me as I don't want them to go to the French lawyers till I know what's in them?'

'It all sounds most intriguing Peter. One of our junior partners took a French degree before reading law – I'm certain she could look after it for you unless, of course, you want a literal translation in which case I could pass it to the agency that handles all our legal requirements in French.'

'I'm sure that won't be necessary, can I drop them in on Monday.'

'Yes, I'm in meetings during the morning but I'll tell my secretary to expect them and in the meantime I'll brief my colleague to provide you with a decent summary of the contents of the files and also of the letters.'

'As I shan't be seeing you on Monday I should just mention one thing in confidence. Apart from the letters, all of which appear to be from the same woman and are signed in comparatively intimate terms, there are also some postcards from a child who addresses Pierre as "Cher Oncle".'

'Good Lord,' said Richard. 'What on earth can that mean?'

'I can't imagine, but I guess we'll have a better idea next week.'

When he got back to his flat, Peter decided to take a closer look at the photographs and the letters. Many of them were quite short but one was much longer. There were no addresses at the tops, merely the dates and, in the longer one, an indentation in the top left hand corner that was also evident on the second page, suggesting there may have been an attachment.

He laid out the photographs on a table and then noticed that the photograph of the young woman with the baby also had an indentation in the top left hand corner. He went back to the letter and placed it over the photograph and found that the marks were identical. 'So that photograph accompanied the letter when it was sent to Pierre all those years ago,' thought Peter. 'Who are they and what is this all about?'

As it was now getting late, he decided to postpone any further speculation about Pierre's possessions until he had a better idea of the contents of the files and letters. However, the more he reflected on what he had discovered, the more he felt compelled to talk to Mark Carter. 'I'll ring him tomorrow,' thought Peter. 'He must know something about these photographs and what they all mean.'

The next morning Peter had a call from Mike Docherty.

'Were you able to get anything helpful from those letters and files?'

'Unfortunately the combination of faded and somewhat unreadable writing and my poor French means I'll have to get someone else to do it for me. But I'm about to ring Mark Carter and maybe we can get together again if anything relevant comes up.'

'Glad to help – I hope he can throw more light on everything.'

After skipping through the Sunday papers Peter dialled the number Branko had given him.

It rang nearly a dozen times and Peter was about to hang up when an American voice came on the phone.

'Hi, it's Mark here, who's calling?'

'Good morning Mr Carter, my name is Peter Barton and I am Pierre Vaillant's nephew. Sadly he died last year and I'm helping the lawyers to sort out a few loose ends in connection with his estate. I believe you first met him during the war and kept in touch once it was over. I was wondering if you could fill in some gaps in the information I've been able to gather about what he was doing in France during the war and also whether you could tell me anything about someone called Delphine who was corresponding with him.'

'Gee, I'm really sorry to hear your news. He was a good friend but we kind of lost touch a while ago. I guess you must be Veronique's boy. I think I met you once when you were about six or seven at Pierre's place in London but once he went back to France we didn't see much of each other after that. By the way, the name's Mark. Sure I can help you, although my memory's not as sharp as it used to be. It's a very long story, Peter, so maybe the best thing would be for us to meet. Where are you calling from?'

'I live in London,' said Peter, 'but I could come down to Milborne Port.'

'That's not necessary, I get up to London a couple of times a month to meet up with some buddies. How would Wednesday suit you – say after lunch?'

'That's great,' said Peter. 'Why don't we meet at my flat?'

'Sure if it's reasonably central – can you email the address and also some directions as I don't have a London road map?'

'I'll do it right away and if you have any problems just give me a ring.'

On Monday morning Peter dropped off the files and letters at his solicitor's office. 'Any idea how long it'll take?' he asked Richard Anstruther's secretary.

'I believe Richard is planning to see his colleague later this afternoon, I am sure he'll let you know once he's discussed it with her.'

Peter returned to his flat and looked again at the remaining contents of the holdalls, none of which seemed to have any significance. It was clear that the photographs were meaningless until he saw Mark Carter. He assumed the medals and the revolver were relics from the war, whilst the boxes contained small personal items – cufflinks, collar studs, a silver propelling pencil, an empty wallet embossed with the initials 'PLV', eight old one hundred franc notes and a few of smaller denominations and what looked like a key to a safe deposit box with the initials

'BNP' stamped on it. 'Might that be Banque Nationale de Paris?' he wondered, 'and if so where?'

Peter's thoughts were interrupted by the phone.

'Hello Peter, it's Suzanne. Are you having any success?'

Peter decided to reveal nothing about his trip to Berwick St James.

'Not really. I'm trying to find out more about Pierre's wartime activities but it's not proving easy. Has the lawyer in Nice made any further progress?'

'I'm not aware of any but Maman may have more news, she keeps in fairly close touch with him. Shall I ask her?'

'No, I just wondered. By the way, do you by any chance recall whether Pierre ever had a bank account with BNP?'

'Not as far as I know. I think the vineyard account was with Crédit Agricole and I believe his personal account was with Société Générale. Why do you ask?'

'No special reason – I just couldn't remember who he banked with.'

'When are you likely to be coming back to Nice?'

'I'm not sure, maybe later in the month.'

'Let me know when you'll be here so we can meet up.'

'I look forward to it, thanks for calling.'

Later in the day, Richard Anstruther called.

'Just getting back to you about the translations – my colleague is pretty busy with due diligence on a takeover bid but she knows it's urgent and will fit it in as quickly as possible. I've asked her to give priority to the letters. Why don't you give me a call later in the week if I haven't got back to you?'

'Thanks Richard. Tell me, do you feel that your opposite number in France is keeping you fully up to date with their activities?'

'More or less. I have the impression they're very anxious to finalise matters and sort out the inheritance tax issue so that they can close their files. Maybe once we've had a look at those letters and the files, we can give them what they require.'

'I certainly hope so. In the meantime, I thought you might be interested to know that I spoke to Mark Carter and mentioned the letters from Delphine. He said it's a very long story so we're meeting later in the week. Maybe then I can get a better idea of what Pierre was doing during the war and also what bearing it has on tying up the loose ends of his estate. Perhaps most important, he can tell me who is writing to Pierre as "Dear Uncle".'

'I wish I could be a fly on your wall when you meet,' said Richard. 'However, I must go as a client has just arrived for a meeting.'

A couple of days later, after he had finished lunch, Peter found himself pacing up and down in his flat waiting for Mark Carter. He had put the photographs, the medals, the revolver and the various keys on a side table so that he could ask Mark about them. It was now after four and he was beginning to wonder whether Mark had forgotten the appointment or couldn't find the flat. 'I should have asked if he had a mobile phone,' thought Peter. 'Although I suspect that would be unlikely.'

Ten minutes later the doorbell rang.

Peter opened it and found a tall, slim blue eyed man with white crew cut hair.

'You must be Mark,' he said as they shook hands.

'That's right,' came back the reply with a slight trace of a southern American accent. 'I'm real sorry to be late but I guess the lunch ran on longer than I'd planned and then I somehow took a couple of wrong turns on my way over here. But it's great to see you and I hope the delay hasn't thrown you out.'

'It's not a problem,' said Peter. 'I was keeping myself free as you said you had a long story to tell. Why don't we make ourselves comfortable in my study?'

He ushered Mark into a small room with books on two walls, a leather topped desk and three comfortable armchairs which appeared to have enjoyed a good deal of use. A window, through which the sun was coming at an angle over the top of some evergreen shrubs, looked out onto the rear garden.

'This is mighty pleasant,' said Mark. 'Looks like you're a big reader.'

'Most are my own, but I inherited some and a few have been given to me over the years by friends. I wish I found more time for reading, but nowadays it seems to be a luxury one can only indulge in on holiday.'

'It's one of the pleasures of retirement – I find it very relaxing, particularly biographies, and especially those about the leaders who influenced events during and after the war.'

'It's what happened to Pierre in the war, as well as after it ended, that I wanted to ask you about. Do you mind telling me as much as you can remember about how you met and also what you know about his time in France around the time the war ended? But before we start can I get you a drink?'

'Well, if it isn't too early a small Scotch and water would be real nice.'

Peter poured a drink for Mark and a weaker one for himself.

'All the best and thanks for coming.'

'My pleasure,' said Mark. 'Shall I start by telling you when and where we met?'

'Please do,' said Peter.

'OK, so here's how it was. In late 1943 I started my flying training at Austin, Texas, which lasted for nearly two months. Part of the training involved dropping paratroopers and towing gliders, the reason for which became clear later. My buddies and I completed our training early in 1944 and we then waited for the delivery of our planes. After two or three weeks of familiarisation, we were told we would be flying to North Africa via Ascension Island. It was a tiring nine-hour flight and we had to have additional tanks for fuel to give us extra range, but we made it.

'After a few days on Ascension, we took off on another long flight to Liberia and finally the last leg that took us to Marrakech. That was some place. Many different nationalities, mostly Arabs, many of whom worked for the Germans as spies or fifth columnists. That's where I first came across Pierre, who seemed to be involved in some sort of surveillance operation. We first met in one of the city's many clubs. He was young, charming, spoke good English, had plenty of money and was always in the company of interesting people – Arabs, Maltese, Greeks and a couple of other Frenchmen, often with attractive Arab girls who I guess were used to get information from the Germans.

'Many of the others were involved in black market activities and seemed to be making a lot of money. One of my buddies was our navigator called Ted Docherty and he and Pierre became very friendly with two particular Arab girls – they all spent a lot of time together. We certainly had a lot of fun, but after about ten days we were told we were to fly on to England where we would be based.

'When Pierre heard about this from Ted he asked if he could fly back with us as he needed to make a report about his activities and was anxious to get to London as soon as possible. I had a word with our squadron commander who gave us the OK once he had checked Pierre's papers and had a positive clearance from his Free French controllers in London.

'Ted and I guessed Pierre was in North Africa on an intelligence gathering operation but he always seemed very reluctant to talk about anything, other than to say he was making contacts. Anyway we left Marrakech with Pierre on board early the following morning heading out towards Casablanca and on into the Atlantic to avoid the risk of German fighters based on the west coast of France. We flew out over the sea for several hours before turning north -east towards England. We then headed along the Channel before sending a coded message to our future base in southern England. I remember that we had trouble decoding the message from the RAF operator – they transmitted much faster than us – but we finally came down on a runway that was almost too short for our plane. We pulled up just before we ran out of tarmac. Seems we were on the wrong runway but, heck, we were down in one piece! We got out, jumped into a jeep and took off for the mess to get some breakfast with Pierre in tow. The last thing I remember was the arrival of a bunch of female mechanics to check over the plane – we hoped they knew what they were doing!

'After debriefing and a great English breakfast, Pierre said he had to take off as he had managed to get a lift with an RAF officer who had to attend a meeting with some high-ups in London. He gave us a phone number where we could get in touch and said that if we got a twenty-four hour pass he would buy us dinner in the West End. Meanwhile we were busy flying various missions in northern France and Holland without encountering too many problems and when we weren't flying, we enjoyed the many pretty pubs and attractive girls in the area around our base.

'Towards the end of May, when we had been at the base for about a month, our flight commander briefed us that we would be flying on a mission the following night which would involve dropping saboteurs and British and French agents into France to work with the French Resistance. The next night we went out to our plane to find a group of what appeared to be civilian workers waiting for us, loaded down with huge rucksacks. Who should be among them but Pierre! We started the engines and took off at around 11pm. After flying for about half an hour, Pierre came forward to talk to Ted and me. He told us that he was to meet with local Resistance chiefs, brief them about D-Day and plan a sabotage programme designed to create as much chaos as possible before the Invasion. He wasn't sure how long he would be in France but felt confident he would have no problems as he had a good cover story and would be staying with a local family whose daughter, Delphine, was in touch with all the key people he had to contact. We wished him well and agreed we would meet up again in London to celebrate once the war was over.

'Shortly afterwards we were nearing the drop zone when we were hit in the tail by anti-aircraft fire. We managed to keep on flying but were losing altitude fast and were mighty relieved when we saw lights flashing in a prearranged sequence down below. We circled to give the guys in the back time to prepare to jump and a couple of minutes later they were gone.

'We now had our own problems and I realised we were losing height so fast we would have to make a crash-landing. Luckily, I saw an area of what looked like pasture and decided it was our best hope despite what appeared to be a heavily wooded area up ahead. You don't get to practice crash-landings in the USAF but as they go, it could have been a lot worse. The undercarriage was a hell of a mess and the tip of one of the wings broke off, but we scrambled out of the plane and were relieved that our radio operator had managed to send a signal saying that although the plane was shot up we were OK and would try to ditch wherever we could.'

At this point Mark stopped. 'I told you it was a long story, do you want me to go on.'

'If you're happy to,' said Peter. 'But how about another drink?'

'That'd be swell.'

'Before you continue, can I just ask whether you got the impression that Pierre had been operating in the area previously and knew the people who he'd be staying with?'

'It's possible, but we had very little time to talk before he jumped.'

Peter poured another couple of glasses and handed one to Mark.

'Gee, thanks Peter, this is really great Scotch – almost as good as Bourbon! So here we were in Occupied France with very little idea of our exact location other than being around three or four minutes flying time from the drop point. Ted did some basic calculations and estimated that we were about ten miles further east of our target in what appeared to be a heavily wooded country. We started walking in the direction of the original map reference point and were making good progress when suddenly torches were shone on us from a number of different directions and we found ourselves surrounded by a group of villainous looking Frenchmen armed with some serious firepower. After explaining what had happened to our plane and that we were trying to re-establish contact with the guys we had just dropped, the leader told us in a combination of broken English and sign language that he knew the place we were trying to reach and that he would lead us there.

'So suddenly things are looking up! He took us to a barn and came back after a few minutes with clothes for Ted and me as well as for my co-pilot, the wireless operator and our two gunners. He also produced a couple of bottles of wine and some bread and cheese. Mighty welcome it was too! After we had changed, he indicated that we should split into two groups. Ted and I with Hank, one of the gunners, would go with him, the others would go with his brother. So we set off across country in order to reach our destination before daylight. We were bushed but we got to the outskirts of a smallish village just before dawn and were shown into another large barn. We climbed a ladder which was then removed and bedded down to try to get some sleep. Before our guide left us he pointed to eight on his watch and signed that someone would bring us some food.

'The next morning we were awoken by a familiar voice. It was Pierre! After Ted and I explained what had happened to us, Pierre said he'd try to organise a way to get us out of France, but that he had to meet with a number of local Resistance leaders in a nearby village and wouldn't be back until the following day as it was inadvisable to be out at night unless it was absolutely crucial. He then told us that Delphine, who headed the local cell, had already arranged for all the key people to attend the meeting and would go with him to establish his bona fides, but she would then return to start planning our escape route either to the north by sea or else across the Pyrenees to Spain and then back to England. He emphasised that with the imminence of the invasion of France we had to get away from the area fast, as it would be awash with German troops reinforcing their front line and that

Delphine would try to set up connections with others who could help us. Needless to say, we were mighty relieved when he said they could help us get back home. He told us to keep absolutely quiet until we heard a particular sequence of notes being whistled which would signify that we were being brought some food. He then left.

'Around lunchtime some soup and rolls and a bottle of wine were brought to us and later in the afternoon we heard the same whistle and were greeted by a very pretty French girl wearing shapeless dungarees and a headscarf. Dark haired with brown eyes, she looked no more than seventeen or eighteen but we guessed she must be older as she had a very confident manner which gave an impression of quiet authority. She told us she was Delphine and explained she'd already been in touch with contacts who'd helped numerous RAF flyers to escape and hoped to be able to get us on our way within a couple of days. We slept a bit, then in the evening Delphine returned with more food. She had bad news. Our other crew members had run into a German patrol. They'd made a run for it and one of them had been wounded, the other two captured. She was concerned that our captured colleagues would reveal that other crew members were hiding locally which would lead to a search, so she'd try to arrange for us to be moved as soon as Pierre got back the next day.

'We had a restless night and thought we heard the sound of armoured vehicles approaching but in the end we weren't disturbed. The next morning, Delphine appeared with Pierre. He looked very tired but was in good spirits as his meetings had all been very successful and the plans that had been developed in London for sabotaging railways and bridges had all been finalised. Delphine said that her contacts would be coming for us that night and would accompany us for the next two days when we'd be handed over to other members of the pipeline who'd get us to the Spanish border. The route north to the coast was too dangerous because of German patrols. She estimated that by walking around six hours at night it would take us approximately three weeks to get to our destination and then on to England. Pierre seemed in a hurry so he left us saying he'd return later with some lunch.

'When he came back we had a chance to ask him a bit more about the role he'd be playing when the Invasion commenced.

He was fairly tight-lipped as I guess he was worried what might happen if we were caught and questioned by the Gestapo. However, we got the impression he was one of a number of French nationals who'd been based in London for about a year, gathering information on various fronts to gauge enemy manpower and deployment and that their role would be to harass the Germans in any way they could by acts of sabotage once the Invasion started. Ted and I were both immensely impressed by the courage that he and Delphine displayed in facing such overwhelming odds, particularly as she was so young.

'After talking more about the route we'd be taking and the people who'd be accompanying us, Pierre said he had to go and left saying very confidently that we'd meet up again in London when the war was over. As he departed, he thanked us quite emotionally for the part our country was playing in helping to liberate France.

'We were desperate to smoke but Delphine had told us not to and had destroyed our American cigarettes. She came back in the afternoon with some French ones and we smoked whilst they kept a lookout, but she stressed that we shouldn't smoke again until we'd left. Foul smelling and even worse tasting, we all agreed they were as good a reason as any to want to get back to the PX store at our base!'

Just then the phone rang. Peter did not answer but he heard Richard Anstruther's voice on the answerphone.

'Peter, I have translations of the letters and the contents of one are of huge significance. I thought I should ring you immediately – call me back as soon as you can.'

Mark looked at his watch. 'Do you want to call him back? I'm meant to meet a buddy for a drink at 7.15 and I really should be going. I could get together with you in the morning to tell you the rest of the story if you like – I'm not getting the train till 2.20 in the afternoon.'

'If you can spare the time that'd be really kind,' said Peter. 'Where are you staying?'

'The Cadogan Hotel in Knightsbridge. I reckon it'll take another half an hour for me to finish the story but you may have some questions.'

'Quite a few already but they can keep till the morning. Shall I come to your hotel at 9.15?'

'That'd be fine. It'll give me time to take a look round Harrods's food department and pick up a few things I can't get in Milborne Port before I get the train.'

After Mark had gone, Peter called Richard Anstruther.

'I've just picked up your call. You said there was something of great significance in the letters.'

'Peter, it's a bit of a bombshell. Apparently a child was born as a result of the relationship your uncle had with the Frenchwoman who signed herself Delphine. It's quite a complicated story. Would you like me to go through the letters now or do you want to pop in to the office tomorrow?'

For a few moments Peter was speechless, then he slowly reacted.

'I can't believe it Richard – how absolutely extraordinary.'

The news, coupled with Mark's revelations about Pierre's wartime activities suddenly left Peter feeling completely drained.

'If you don't mind Richard, I think I'd prefer to talk to you about it tomorrow as it's very difficult to take in and I'm feeling rather tired. I've spent the last couple of hours with an American, called Mark Carter, who met Pierre during the war and he's been telling me something about Pierre's clandestine activities in France just prior to D-Day. I also know a little about Delphine, who was a local Resistance fighter. I'm seeing Mark again first thing tomorrow morning – would it be convenient if we met after that so that I can read the letters?'

'That would be fine. How about coming in for a cup of coffee at eleven o'clock?'

'I'll see you then.'

Peter went back and sprawled in the armchair he had just vacated and tried to take in the significance of Richard's news, coupled with what Mark had told him about Pierre's activities in France. He wondered what more Mark might reveal and also how he and his two crew members managed to get back to England. Was Delphine still alive – she must be in her seventies – and what of the child who had written to Pierre? Where might they be now and would the files he had left with Richard throw even more light on these extraordinary revelations?

He decided it would be futile to speculate further until he talked again to Mark, but he felt instinctively that whatever arose he should say nothing about his conversation with Richard when they met.

CHAPTER FOUR

THE NEXT MORNING he was at the Cadogan Hotel just after nine. Mark met him in reception and showed him through to a comfortable lounge and ordered coffee for both of them.

'Shall I try to pick up the story where I broke off yesterday?' said Mark.

'That'd be perfect.'

'OK, so I think I told you Pierre had to leave, as he had to press on with his assignment, and that Delphine was to accompany us on the first stage of our trek to the Spanish border.'

'That's right,' replied Peter. 'And you also mentioned some very unpleasant French cigarettes.'

'I can almost taste them still but at least we had our first smoke for a couple of days! Anyway when it was dark, Delphine came over to the barn with a couple of the guys we'd seen previously and explained the plan. We'd cover as much ground as possible at night and would then rest up between daybreak and nightfall in farm buildings owned by trusted contacts along the route. She was confident all would be well, as the system had been used many times during the previous four years and there had never been a problem.

'So we set out, walking fairly fast, sticking to woods, fields and country footpaths, which she seemed to know well. We occasionally heard vehicles which must have been German as there was a curfew, but otherwise we had no problems and arrived at our next destination well before sunrise having covered nearly twenty miles. When we got there, we were given food, water and some wine which Delphine shared with us before saying she'd have to leave, as Pierre needed her help in organising a major sabotage exercise planned for the following evening. She left after giving each of us a hug and a kiss as well as another packet of the same unpleasant French cigarettes! We were all secretly in love with her and hoped that the plans she and Pierre were making would be successful.

'Meanwhile, we pushed ahead night after night making good time and found ourselves close to the Spanish border just over three weeks after we set out. Our guides knew an area where surveillance was minimal and we crawled across having negotiated some barbed wire and avoided a powerful searchlight that continuously swept across us. We went on into a small town and were taken to a cheap hotel where we had our first decent meal for days and were shown to a room with three beds. We were in seventh heaven!

'That night we slept like logs and after breakfast the next day we went by truck to a small town by the sea where we waited a few more days before boarding a fishing boat. We were at sea for five days and narrowly avoided German patrol boats, one of which came extremely close but, after an exchange by loudhailer, they let us proceed. At the time the nets were being hauled in so I guess everything looked authentic. I sure as hell appreciated being a flyer after that experience – it was terrible. We were sick most of the time and were mighty relieved to come ashore somewhere in south-west England. We finally arrived back at our base around the middle of July and caught up on all the news about the success of the Normandy landings.

'I guess there's not a lot more to tell. Our buddies had flown hundreds of sorties in support of the Allied troops, dropping equipment and flying out wounded from captured airfields. Ted and I soon resumed duty and joined them on these mercy missions when we would pick up American, British and French servicemen and occasionally wounded French men and women who must have been agents working with the Resistance. We remembered one of them from the group we had dropped nearly two months before. We asked him about Pierre but he had no news, although he did tell us that Delphine had been captured and taken away for questioning. Nobody had heard anything more about her after that.

'A few weeks later we took part in "Operation Market Garden", dropping paratroops and towing gliders over to Holland, where a huge battle was taking place around Arnhem and Nijmegen. Sadly, that was something of a disaster but the war was going our way and, towards the end of 1944, we were transferred to a base in northern France where we flew sorties in support of our troops fighting in the Ardennes. One evening we were sitting in a local bar when we saw a group of Frenchmen in the midst of what appeared to be a celebration. One of them was Pierre!

'Ted and I went over and both of us gave him a huge bear hug. "What's going on – has the war ended?" I asked him. "No," he replied, "one of my friends is getting married on the weekend and we're celebrating." He asked us about our escape and what we were doing in France and told us about his work behind enemy lines in the days prior to and the weeks immediately after D-Day. He and other members of his group had been responsible for sabotaging railroads, bridges and supply dumps and following the Invasion, as their numbers grew, they'd been involved in direct guerrilla style battles with the Germans. I then enquired whether he had any news about Delphine. His tone changed and it was obvious he was distressed at the mention of her name. He told us about an incident when part of his group had been preparing to attack retreating German troops a couple of months after the Invasion. Delphine was driving a car with three others when they were stopped by a German patrol not far from a bridge they had just blown. The men had engaged the Germans in a gun fight whilst she'd tried to get away. Two of her compatriots had been killed, one wounded and she had been captured.

'Pierre had tried to find out what had happened to her without success. He feared she may have been tortured to reveal information about her colleagues and then removed to a concentration camp. Apparently, he bribed some Vichy officials to try to get information and was almost caught by the Gestapo, but managed to elude them and was moved to the Caen area to get away from the immediate vicinity. Since September he'd been working with Free French officials in the area trying to re-establish order in the wake of the vacuum created by the departure of the Germans and the downfall of the Vichy Government.

'We asked him about his future plans. He said he was hoping to get back to England once France was more stable as he had a number of good friends in London and was looking forward to catching up with them. Ted and I got the impression he might have been a bit of a ladies' man when we met him in Marrakech and thought there might be a girlfriend in London waiting for his return. However, we had to leave as we were scheduled to fly again that night but agreed to meet for dinner later in the week. Meanwhile, we continued flying across northern Europe and occasionally attacking convoys of German armour inside Germany itself.

'We met a number of times after that and Pierre always seemed to have plenty of money. I remember commenting that liberation appeared to suit him as he was extremely generous whenever we got together. We celebrated New Year's Day in 1945 by meeting for dinner in a charming restaurant overlooking a very pretty river. Pierre recommended the trout which he said were caught there each day. I'm a fisherman myself so I thought that was a good suggestion and so it proved. We drank a great deal of local wine and Pierre said that one day he would like to own a vineyard but it would have to be in the south because the climate in the north didn't suit him. We all speculated about when the war would finish and Pierre became quite emotional about how much he appreciated our friendship and said he hoped we'd continue to see each other when it was all over.

'About a week later, Pierre came to our base to tell us he was finally returning to England and gave us an address in London where we could contact him. That's more or less the end of the story. We continued flying sorties into Germany and were bringing back more wounded and newly released POWs when we heard on the radio that the war was over. A couple of weeks later we got back to England and we had something of a surprise. One evening, Ted and I decided to call Pierre at the number he had given us. A female voice answered and said "Hello, it's Mary here". I asked if Pierre was there and I heard her calling Pierre to the phone. We arranged to get together as planned at the Café Royal the following evening.

'We met up in the bar and after a few drinks sat down to dinner, at which point Pierre told us that he and Mary had got married two or three months earlier. At first, Ted and I couldn't believe it, but Pierre told us he had known Mary for more than a year, that they were engaged before he left for France and had always intended to get married when he returned to England. We talked a great deal about the future and he asked us what we planned to do now the war was over. I told him I was thinking of settling in England, as I liked the country and had become attached to an English girl who I was hoping to marry. Ted wasn't sure of his plans but Pierre gave us the impression he had a number of potential business interests he was intending to develop and talked about the possibility of us doing something together.

'Both Ted and I were really pleased to see him again, but we both agreed afterwards that he hadn't seemed as cheerful or upbeat as we had previously remembered him – he seemed somewhat subdued and we wondered whether his marriage was not working out as well as he'd hoped.'

Peter interrupted him to ask, 'Did he say anything more about what might have happened to Delphine?'

'I asked him whether he had any news about her. He said he'd heard rumours from some of his ex-Resistance contacts that she might be alive but he had no real information. She'd been involved in many operations in the weeks following D-Day and had been lucky, as when she was captured she wasn't armed and had claimed she'd been forced to drive the vehicle. Apparently, she was interrogated for days but she revealed nothing and after threats she would be shot, she was sent to a camp from which she was finally freed early in 1945. I got the impression he felt responsible for what had happened to her even though he was not involved in the events when she was caught. He then changed the subject and started talking again about business and the opportunities we might develop together.'

Peter opened his wallet and took out the photographs he had found among Pierre's papers.

'I found these among a number of items that were stored by Pierre in a barn at the property where Ted Docherty's son Mike now lives.'

'Over at Berwick St James?'

'Yes,' said Peter. 'He stored a few personal items there but obviously never came back to retrieve them. I assume these two photos are of you and Ted with Pierre?'

'Would you believe it? These must have been taken towards the end of 1944 when we'd been posted to a base in northern France and met up with Pierre again.'

'One of them is dated New Year's Day 1945.'

'Why yes, that's where we met for dinner at that great little restaurant I told you about, the one overlooking a river. Pierre insisted that Ted and I have the trout, which was a specialty and it was absolutely delicious.'

'Do you recognise this picture?' said Peter passing over the photographs of the young woman.

'Of course, that's Delphine. Who are the baby and the small child?'

'I don't know,' said Peter. 'They may have been her relatives.'

'I assume Mary knew nothing about Pierre having these – I always thought she was the jealous type as she kept a close eye on Pierre when young women were around.'

'I've no idea, but he was obviously keen to keep them tucked away from prying eyes.'

'So Delphine was eventually in touch with him after she was released – he never mentioned anything about that to me, or Ted either, as far as I know.'

'I guess she must have been,' said Peter. He looked at his watch and realised he would have to hurry to get to his meeting with Richard Anstruther on time.

'I'm afraid I'll have to be going, Mark, as I'm due to be at another meeting in fifteen minutes. I'm immensely grateful to you for filling in all this background about Pierre – I really feel I now know him a lot better than when he was alive. Had there been more time I was hoping to talk to you about Pierre's activities after the war but maybe we could do that on another occasion.'

'I'd be happy to and I've enjoyed reminiscing about events I'd almost forgotten. It's been great meeting you and I hope we can get together again real soon.'

'Just before I go could I ask you just one other thing? You don't know by any chance whether Pierre had a bank account with BNP?'

'Yes, I think he had an account in the City – somewhere like Moorgate or London Wall.'

'Mark, you've been a great help – perhaps we could meet up again when next you're in town.'

'That'd be fine – as I mentioned, I normally come up at least once a month to meet buddies but of course you're very welcome to pop in to see me if you're anywhere near my part of the world.'

'I might just do that, but meanwhile, thank you again.'

Peter managed to grab a cab as he left the hotel and immediately decided he should have found time to talk more about Mark's impressions of Pierre's relationship with Mary in the early years of their marriage. Clearly the news of Delphine having a child would have been a bombshell to Pierre, coming as it must have done such a short time after his marriage. Could he possibly have known Delphine was pregnant before he got married? How had he managed to keep it from Mary throughout their marriage and had he ever seen Delphine again and met his daughter? Might Mary have known, or else found out about Delphine? These and countless other thoughts whirred around in his head en route to meet Richard Anstruther.

When he reached his solicitor's office he was shown to a meeting room, offered coffee, which he declined, and was told that Mr Anstruther would not keep him more than a minute or two. Whilst waiting, Peter started looking at the firm's brochure, but Richard was as punctual as his secretary had suggested and came into the room smiling.

'Good morning Peter. I do hope you've been offered coffee.'

'I was and I declined thank you Richard, I've already had far too many cups this morning. So what have you been able to find out?'

Richard poured a cup of coffee and added two spoonfuls of sugar. 'You don't mind if I have one I hope – I've been in meetings since seven o'clock this morning and feel in need of something to give me a lift.'

Richard passed three translations across the table. 'I think the longest one will be of greatest interest.'

Dated March 20, 1945 it read as follows.

My Dearest Pierre,

I am hoping this letter will eventually reach you, although I still have no idea where you may be. I am entrusting it to a Free French officer who will be attending a meeting in London next week and has promised to try to locate you – he believes you may now have settled England.

I have no idea whether you received the letters I wrote in January and February after I was liberated from the camp where I had been held for many months. Pierre, my darling, we have a baby daughter who I have decided to call Juliette. She has your eyes, a charming little nose and also a dimple that she has inherited from me! She is a wonderful, happy child and was born ten days ago. I am sure you will be enchanted with her and in the meantime am enclosing a photograph so you can see how beautiful she is.

Without any news about you, the time I spent in the camp was unbearable. I missed you so much and feared I would never see you again but when I realised I was pregnant I was full of hope and one of the guards even showed me a little kindness when my condition could no longer be hidden.

I pray you are well and we will soon be reunited – you can write to me at my parents' home as I am staying with them until I can find a room of my own. My mother will then look after Juliette so that I can get work, which should not be too difficult now that life in France is getting a little easier.

We hear that the war should soon be over – I so look forward to being with you again my dearest and for us to be able to share life together with our beautiful gift from God.

Please write soon I am desperate for news of you,

All my love,
Delphine

x

The next was somewhat shorter and dated 27 January 1945.

Dearest Pierre,

I am alive and have just been released from the camp where I have been held for the last five months. Yesterday American troops were rumoured to be no more than eight miles away and within hours the guards had fled. It has been very hard but I have survived and wanted you to know as soon as possible that you will soon be a father as I am expecting a baby. I hope it will not come as a complete surprise.

I am so happy darling, but I am also fearful as I have no idea where you are. One of my fellow prisoners came into the camp in November and gave me news that you had moved further to the west, helping to restore order around Caen following the devastation caused in the battle for control of the city.

I hope this reaches you soon and that all is well. I am relying on Jean, who survived the many round-ups, to find a way of getting it to you as he believes he knows where you may be.

Pierre, I long to be with you again – please write to me soon, care of my family as I shall stay with them till the baby is born.

With all my love,
Delphine

x

Another even shorter letter was dated 15 February.

My Darling Pierre,

I have still heard nothing from you and am desperate for news. In case you did not get my previous letter, I am writing again to tell you that I am expecting our baby around the middle of next month. I am very excited, but also anxious, because I have no idea where you are or how to get in touch with you.

I pray that all is well with you and that the package is still safe wherever you hid it after the events of that extraordinary night.

I am missing you terribly and am longing for news – please write soon,

Your loving Delphine

x

Peter finished reading and passed over one of the photographs he had been examining in his study. 'Well Richard, at first I could hardly believe the news you gave me on the telephone but one thing is a little clearer – this must be the baby to whom Delphine is referring in her letters.'

'Where did you find this photograph?'

'It was in the box of items in Berwick St James.'

'So Pierre did ultimately become aware of Delphine's situation and of the birth of his child, but of course we don't know when.'

'No, we don't, but it must have been some time after the last letter was sent, otherwise I can't believe he would have gone ahead with his marriage. When he received the letters, it must have been a terrible shock to find out he was a father, the more so as he had so recently got married.'

'My colleague also took a look through the postcards but there is nothing of significance in them. As you know they are addressed "Dear Uncle" but merely refer to being at various different places and sending greetings from them – very much the sort of thing that children send when on holiday.'

'That does suggest that there must have been contact between Pierre and Delphine after the child was born, otherwise Juliette wouldn't have been writing to him.'

'I agree – maybe the files will be more revealing, particularly about the mysterious package.'

'Do you have any idea how long those translations might take?'

'There are quite a lot of them – I suspect they'll take at least a week unless we simply summarise the contents at first.'

'Richard, I think that would be ideal for now - you've been most helpful as always, I'll await your call.'

CHAPTER FIVE

WHEN PETER GOT back to his flat, he reread the translations and tried to imagine what effect they would have had on his uncle. They would obviously have come as a considerable shock but it was equally clear that Pierre's ex-wife had no knowledge of Delphine or of the relationship that had existed between the two of them before Delphine was captured. If Juliette knew Pierre as 'Uncle' she must have met him on a number of occasions. He looked again at the dates on the cards, the first of which was sent in 1951. So Pierre must have been in France and met her at least once before then. How could he find out more and also where Delphine, if she was still alive, and Juliette were now living? He also needed to know Delphine's surname if he was ever going to trace her.

Although he felt that the files would ultimately reveal more about what had happened after the war, Peter was impatient to try to get answers to the many questions that remained unresolved. He decided to give Mike Docherty a call.

'Hello Mike, I was hoping to catch you, do you have a moment?'

'Sure thing, what's on your mind?'

'Well, I've had a couple of long talks with Mark Carter and now know something about the time he and your dad were in Occupied France after their plane crashed and also how, with Pierre's help, they managed to escape and get back to England. There are still a lot more unanswered questions and I was wondering whether by any chance your father had kept any of his personal correspondence from that time and, more importantly, whether there is anything to indicate that Pierre went back to the area around Caen after the war and what he might have been doing there.'

'There's a load of stuff up in the attic that I haven't looked at since Dad died. If you like, I'll go through it and see if I can find anything.'

'That'd be really kind – I'm particularly interested in anything which suggests Pierre was in that part of France between 1946 and 1950.'

'Leave it with me. It won't take long, if there is anything of interest up there I'll give you a call back.'

Having thought a little more, Peter called Pierre's ex-wife.

'I'm sorry to bother you Mary, but I'm trying to get a bit more of a picture of Pierre's activities just after the war, which I believe is about the time you got married.'

'Yes we were married in February 1945, almost immediately after he got back from France. We had a very brief honeymoon, a weekend at The Grand in Eastbourne, and then he was back to a desk job in London with some of de Gaulle's people. I think he found it a relief after the stresses of work with the Resistance in France but he was always talking about setting up in business, doing exporting and importing. He had some good connections in North Africa through a Croat called Goran Dantic and planned to import rugs, pottery and other local wares to sell through a craft shop in the West End.'

'Did he go back to France very often after you got married?'

'We went to the south of France for a proper honeymoon in 1947 and stayed in Nice. Pierre used to say he would like to live there but I preferred England. Apart from that he went to northern France quite often on business trips – amongst other things, I think he used to import farm machinery which he sold to farmers in Lincolnshire, or maybe it was the other way round! He also imported butter and cheese.'

'I suppose you don't know if he ever had a bank account with BNP.'

'Not as far as I can remember. I know he had accounts with Crédit Agricole and Société Générale. He might have done after we were divorced. Why do you ask?'

'No special reason – I think someone mentioned it, maybe Hubert, and I just wanted to make sure there were no more loose ends – thanks again for your help.'

'You could always try asking Mark Carter, I think he and Pierre did quite a lot of business together, so he might remember.'

'I'll make a point of calling him,' said Peter as he rang off.

'So Pierre did go back to northern France,' mused Peter. 'But I wonder where.'

The next morning the phone rang. It was Mike Docherty.

'I've found three letters Pierre sent to Dad from addresses in France. They are postmarked Lisieux and Mondeville. It looks as though Pierre was there doing some business and he mentions a restaurant that apparently he and Dad went to with Mark Carter when they were all in France during the war. In one of them, he refers to someone called Delphine and it ends with Pierre saying she sends her best wishes and hopes she may see my dad in France again some day. Do you know who she is?'

'Yes, she was a member of a French Resistance cell in northern France where Pierre was parachuted to coordinate activity just before and after D-Day. Pierre was in a plane flown by Mark Carter and your dad. It was hit just before Pierre, and the others who were accompanying him, jumped and their plane crash-landed a few minutes later. Some of the crew were captured, but your dad, Mark and one of the air gunners managed to make contact with Pierre and were looked after by the Resistance for a few days before Delphine, who was one of the local leaders, helped them to get across the border to Spain and then back to England. Not long after they left, Delphine was caught up in a firefight and captured by the Germans. She ended up in an internment camp but was released early in 1945 by advancing Allied troops.'

'I have a hazy recollection of my dad mentioning something about his time in France. She sounds quite an impressive young woman.'

'I think she must have been. Having found out about her involvement with Pierre I'm trying to find out whether she's still alive and where she might be living. Is there by any chance anything else in the letters that might indicate where exactly Pierre stayed and also what he was doing there?'

'He talks about importing butter to England where apparently there was still butter rationing, but there are no addresses on the top of the letters, just dates. Wait a minute, I see on the back of one of the envelopes there is a printed address – Hotel de Ville, Monteille.'

'What's the date of the letter?'

'March 8, 1948. The others are dated April 14, 1949, May 6, 1950 and September 24, 1952.'

'Well thanks for that Mike, if I find out anything more about this Delphine I'll let you know.'

'Glad to help, I wish you well.'

Although Mike's information confirmed that Pierre had probably visited Delphine at various times after the war, Peter still did not know where she had been living or anything more about her. Knowing that Pierre was discussing the importation of butter from somewhere near Lisieux and that he had stayed in Monteille over fifty years previously didn't seem to help very much either. He wondered whether it would be worth asking to see the wartime records of the SOE or else Free French operators in the area to try to pinpoint where Delphine had been living and also to find out her surname. However, after further thought, he decided he would have to wait to see what the files might reveal before pursuing that option, since the knowledge that Pierre had visited Delphine after the war persuaded him that their contents must be related to events at that time. He wondered whether the medals would throw any more light on his quest for information but concluded they would only be useful if he contacted the French authorities. He took another look at the pair of candlesticks turning them over to examine the base. There was a faint imprint 'Vigneux et Cie, Caen'.

'I wonder if they are still in business and whether they keep their old records,' thought Peter. 'I suppose they could have been bought by Pierre or perhaps they were given to him as a present. Could they even have been a gift from Delphine?'

He decided to call Mark Carter to see if he could throw any more light on Pierre's business activities after the war.

'Good morning Mark, do you have a few minutes to chat?'

'Sure thing, what's on your mind?'

'Unfortunately I had to rush off the other day before I was able to ask you a bit more about events immediately after the war when I believe you and Pierre did some business together. I wondered whether that was anything to do with importing butter from France, or native crafts from North Africa?'

'Say, you have been doing some homework! Pierre was a real hound dog for spotting an opportunity and trying to exploit it.

He did import butter for a while from a place somewhere near where we were in the war and used to go over there quite often. I think he sold butter and cheese through a chain of grocers called Liptons who are now long gone. He was also doing business in North Africa with a guy called Goran Dantic, who he'd met in Marrakech. Pierre brought a lot of native craft products in from that area and I think he had a pretty good deal going with shops in the West End. I believe everything went OK for a couple of years and then sales started to fall off. However, he also represented a Dutch biscuit company in this country and helped me to get the agency to sell their biscuits in the US. That got me started and a little later I established my own company as a general wholesaler of food products.'

'You said Pierre went over to France fairly frequently – were these trips solely on business or did he and Mary go together?'

'I'm pretty sure he went on his own because Mary wasn't interested in business and he always said his trips involved a lot of entertaining. You know the sort of thing – a few too many drinks, dinner and maybe a nightclub. I don't think Pierre enjoyed doing it but he said it was good for business.'

'Did you ever go to France with him?'

'Yes on one occasion – I think it was in 1949. We went over for a few days and stayed in Caen. Pierre took off to see a couple of contacts but we got together at our favourite restaurant by the river for dinner on the last day.'

'Any idea where he went?'

'Not exactly, he mentioned two or three places that rang a bell from our days there during the war but I can't remember them now.'

'I found a pair of candlesticks among the items stored by Pierre at Ted's old place. They came from a place called Vigneux et Cie in Caen. I don't suppose you know if he bought them himself or whether they were a present to him.'

'I remember them. I think they were a present and I know he was very attached to them. Vigneux was an interesting place. They sold a great deal of silverware, much of it made in their own workshops – I seem to recall that Pierre bought a present for Mary from them during that trip.'

'Did you get the impression that Pierre and Mary had a good relationship in those early years of their marriage?

'I guess so, but they did seem to have fairly frequent bust-ups. I remember one occasion when they came down for the weekend to my place in Milborne Port. There was a huge row about money and Mary accused him of extravagance.'

'In what way?'

'I don't really know, but Mary implied that although Pierre was successful in business he never seemed to give her sufficient money to run the home and spent far too much when he was abroad. Pierre had already developed a pretty expensive lifestyle with a large apartment and a Buick car – he also did a lot of wining and dining in expensive restaurants in Soho. I saw a fair amount of them in the first few years but less so in the sixties – I guess their marriage just got stale.'

'Did they not consider having children?'

'I don't think it was possible. I know Mary wanted a baby but unfortunately she was unable to conceive.'

'That must have been a disappointment for them.'

'Maybe, but Pierre never seemed to give the impression that it concerned him very much.'

'By the way, I meant to ask you whether you can remember Delphine's surname – every time I hear about her it's always by her Christian name.'

'Yes, her surname was Leger.'

'Just one other thing, do you have any recollection of where you dropped Pierre before you crashed all those years ago?'

'Gee, Peter, you ask the damndest questions. Let me think. I know we were told to fly in the direction of the Cherbourg peninsula to avoid night fighters and run along the coast towards Le Havre before turning inland to Caen. At that stage we were only a few minutes from the drop area when we were hit. Fortunately more or less immediately Ted, who was doing the map reading, gave the go ahead for them to jump. We'd been flying due east for maybe seven or eight minutes so I guess they came down no more than thirty miles from Caen. I'm afraid I can't recall the name of our target as we mostly worked on map references, apart from looking out for major landmarks.'

'Mark, you've been a huge help – I'm sorry to have bothered you again.'

'Any time, but the memory isn't like it used to be.'

Peter put down the phone and dug out a detailed map of France. He turned to the Cherbourg peninsula and followed the route of the E46 to Caen. He then spotted Lisieux some fifty miles to the east. Following the road back to Caen he noticed Monteille. With mounting excitement, he recalled his conversation with Mike Docherty. 'That's where Mike said Pierre stayed on one of his trips to France,' he thought. 'Surely this must be very close to where Delphine and her family were living.'

He sat for a while thinking about the information that had emerged. Now he knew Delphine's name and roughly where she had lived it should be possible to trace her. He might even be able to find out more from the silversmith in Caen if she had given Pierre the candlesticks as a present. He decided the only way to deal with the questions that were still unresolved would be to pay a visit to Normandy and try to locate Delphine and possibly Juliette as well.

He picked up the phone to call Richard Anstruther who for once was at his desk.

'Richard, I now know Delphine's surname and have a better idea about where to find her if she's still alive. I'm thinking of paying a visit to Normandy and driving to the area where she must have been living when Pierre first met her, which also seems to be very close to the place from which he was importing cheese and butter. I was thinking of going tomorrow unless you expect to have any more news for me.'

'I don't at this moment, but let me check.'

Peter looked up sailings between Portsmouth and Cherbourg and found there was a regular daily service. He considered booking a hotel but decided against it since he was unsure where he wanted to stay once he was in Normandy. A short while later, Richard called back.

'Not a lot to report. So far all the correspondence seems to be about Pierre's business dealings, mostly with a retailer called Liptons. However my colleague has turned up some invoices and also correspondence with a number of cheese makers in Normandy relating to shipments between 1947 and 1951.'

'Can you give me the names of the manufacturers?'

'Yes, one is called Le Fromagerie in a place called Cambremer, another Fromage et Beurre in La Poste and a third Fromagerie d'Auge in a place called Beuvron-en-Auge.'

'Richard, that's enormously helpful – I suppose there's nothing that gives any hint about the package to which Delphine referred?'

'Sadly not so far, but I have your mobile number and will call as soon as we find anything that appears to be helpful.'

Peter took another look at the map. It was clear that if Pierre was combining his business trips with visits to Delphine and Juliette, they must have lived very close to the road connecting Caen and Lisieux. He decided to waste no further time and to leave for France in the morning.

He slept badly, turning over and over in his mind what he knew about Pierre's activities in France and where he might locate Delphine. Just before six o'clock, he was fully awake and after showering, shaving and having a breakfast of toast and a cup of strong coffee, he was en route to Portsmouth. At that time of the morning, the traffic was reasonably light and, by nine o'clock, he pulled in to the terminal with ample time to catch the 9.30 ferry. Not being a good sailor, Peter hoped it would be a calm crossing.

He found himself a comfortable spot in the lounge and, with plenty of time to read, resigned himself to five hours at sea. The weather was ideal, hazy warm sunshine and a very light breeze that dispelled any fumes from the engines. Peter began to relax and felt sufficiently confident about the negligible swell to have a light lunch in the bar. Shortly afterwards, he made out the French coast on the horizon and was relieved to hear they would be docking at around four o'clock local time.

Peter's car was well positioned to get away quickly and within fifteen minutes of disembarking, he was on the motorway to Caen. On arrival, rather than pushing on, he found a comfortable hotel overlooking gardens in the city centre and booked for two nights.

Feeling in need of some exercise, he took a walk around the area near the hotel. He remembered that much of Caen had been built by William the Conqueror, who had been buried there, but the city had been almost totally destroyed during the war. A look at a guidebook the hotel concierge had given him revealed that as a result of an ambitious rebuilding programme lasting more than ten years, much of the city had finally been restored to its former state. Peter found himself near the ancient Abbaye-aux-Hommes, parts of which were 800 years old, and in contrast to much of the rest of the city still conveyed a strong sense of antiquity. Walking around the outside, he found it difficult to comprehend how a building of such size and magnificence could have been constructed so many centuries previously.

Refreshed by his walk and a glass of Calvados in the hotel's bar, he opened the Caen area telephone directory and quickly found Vigneux et Cie, who were situated not far from the hotel. He then turned to the personal section and looked through the entries for 'D. Leger'. There were a number, with various different second initials and he soon realised that the directory only covered the immediate area around Caen and, rather more worryingly, that Leger was not an uncommon name. As he sat pondering this, he heard the bell at a nearby church signify that it was already eight o'clock so he hurried down to dinner. He was shown to a corner table with a view over the gardens which were now nearly deserted and ordered the chef's special, Sole à la Normande garnished with oysters and mussels and accompanied it with half a bottle of Domaine Bellegarde which the waiter recommended. He decided to follow this with some Camembert and he then had another glass of Calvados with his coffee.

Back in his room, he looked again at the list of those with the name Leger and the initial 'D.' to see if he could tie any of the names more closely to the areas Pierre had visited, but without success. They were all scattered around Caen but none of them were living outside the city or its suburbs. Peter felt very dispirited but he still hoped that the silversmith might be able to help and if not he would try the municipal authorities.

The next morning, he left the hotel immediately after breakfast and walked to the silversmith's, which was in a quiet street in the old part of the city. The premises gave the impression that the business may have been at the same site since its foundation which, according to the engraved glass over the door, was in 1873. The shop was a treasure trove of silverware all displayed in huge glass cases and containing everything from silver candelabra and huge silver sporting cups to goblets, tableware and fine silver jewellery. He approached the counter to be greeted by an impeccably dressed white haired man in his sixties.

'Excuse me Monsieur, do you speak English.'

'Just a little,' came the reply in an accent that suggested false modesty.

'I wonder if you might be able to help me with a rather strange request,' said Peter, taking one of the candlesticks from a bag and putting it on the counter. 'This was purchased from you just after the war and I am trying to trace the person who might have bought it.'

The shop assistant picked up the candlestick and examined it carefully before putting it down.

'Monsieur, I am not sure whether I can help, although it is just possible. I suspect this is one of a pair and would have been specially made for our client as it is not a standard design. If you look at the base you will see very faintly the initials "J. B.". Jean Bursard was one of our craftsmen who worked here until he retired in 1976 – it was he who made this, probably just after the war. If you don't mind waiting, I will look through our records. Do you perhaps know when it was purchased as it may save me a little time?'

'Regrettably no, although it was almost certainly after the war and as you suggest it was one of a pair.'

While the assistant was in an office at the rear of the shop Peter took a closer look at a cabinet which contained a number of beautifully designed items of antique tableware, ranging from large silver ladles to tiny sugar tongs. The dates that accompanied the brief descriptions, coupled with the prices, suggested that each of them was a collector's item. They spanned more than a century and were exquisite examples of their designer's work. He turned his attention to a display case of modern silverware and decided to purchase a paper knife with a handle portraying a leaping leopard as a memento of his visit.

A few minutes later the assistant returned with a large leather bound ledger.

'Monsieur, I find our records show that between 1945 and Jean's retirement we had sixteen orders for these candles, of which five were for pairs. Two of the pairs were purchased by companies in Caen as retirement gifts for their employees, which leaves three other buyers, one of whom was a local collector, who died some years ago. The other purchasers are a M. Vergnol at an address in Bretteville and a company not far from here with whom we have occasionally done business over the years.'

'Can you tell me anything more about these buyers and also where they are located?'

'M. Vergnol means nothing to me. Bretteville is between here and Bayeux. The other purchaser is from the Pays d'Auge area, about 30km east of here.'

'And their name?'

'Fromagerie d'Auge.'

The significance immediately registered with Peter, who then he enquired 'Are they in Beuvron-en-Auge?'

'That's right, the candlesticks were purchased in October 1949 – is that helpful?'

'Immensely, I'm most grateful to you for your help.'

Having bought the paper knife, Peter hurried back to his hotel where he found a message on his mobile phone.

'Peter, it's Richard, can you ring me when you have a moment?'

He dialled Richard and was put through by his secretary.

'Good morning Richard, you asked me to call.'

'Yes Peter, a brief update. We have gone through three of the files so far and the only notable item is an invoice showing that Pierre bought a 2CV Citroën in Caen in 1951. Given his reputation for expensive cars, I can't imagine it was for his personal use, although he may have purchased it for Delphine.'

'It sounds quite possible, particularly as by then Juliette would have been six and Delphine might have needed a car to help her to get about more easily. By the way, I've located the source of the candlesticks – it was purchased by one of the cheese makers with whom Pierre was doing business. I'm hoping that someone there might recall him and even have some idea about Delphine's whereabouts.'

'Bon chance,' said Richard. 'I'll let you know if anything else of interest shows up but it may take a while as there are probably another dozen files to go through.'

Peter went down to his car and took the road out of Caen leading to Lisieux. He soon turned off to Beuvron-en-Auge and found himself flanked by apple orchards and lush green pastures with herds of dairy cows, half-timbered cottages and large manor houses. On his arrival in Beuvron, he was directed to the fromagerie by a local gendarme and a couple of minutes later he pulled into a forecourt at the entrance to what appeared to be an office attached to a warehouse.

After explaining in his limited French that he would like to talk to the propriétaire he was asked to take a seat in a small waiting room adorned with photographs of what he took to be the company's products. A smiling man in his fifties soon appeared, introduced himself as M. Legrand and enquired in excellent English whether Peter had an interest in any particular product.

Peter explained that he was trying to obtain information about business dealings between his uncle and the company in the late 1940s and 1950s and that he was hoping this would help him to trace a local woman who might have been involved in some way with the business dealings between them.

Possibly because Peter was no longer viewed as a potential customer, the smile had long since disappeared, but the proprietor explained that any export dealings at that time would have been handled by his father. He asked for Pierre's name and excused himself after telling an assistant to offer Peter some samples of their cheeses. A plate of Camembert, Pont l'Évêque and two other cheeses with which Peter was not familiar was offered to him, together with some biscuits.

After a while M. Legrand returned once again smiling. 'Good are they not?'

'Excellent, especially the Pont l'Évêque.'

'I have just been talking to my father. He knew your uncle very well and even visited him in England. He would like to talk to you on the phone.'

'Does he speak English?'

'But of course, we have many English customers and he travelled to England on business very frequently.'

M. Legrand's father expressed his sorrow about the news of Pierre Vaillant's death and talked at length about his knowledge of Pierre's wartime activities, having himself been a member of the Resistance. He also mentioned occasions when he and a friend had joined Pierre on some of his clandestine operations. He recalled the business they had subsequently done together, starting in a small way in 1947 and continuing well into the late 1960s by which time Pierre had apparently diversified into other activities. He confirmed that Pierre was a very important and valued customer, that he had paid a number of visits to Beuvron and thought he had probably purchased butter from other suppliers in the area. He remembered Delphine, whom he had met on a number of occasions with Pierre, and on one or two without him when she was handling matters on his behalf. He also knew of her as a member of the Resistance.

'But do you know if she is still alive and where she is living?' said Peter.

'Yes, she is still alive and she lives nearby with her husband who used to be a director of one of the local dairies. They have a small house about half a kilometre away on the road to Repentigny.'

'And do they have any children?'

'No, they married when they were both in their forties, by which time it was not possible for them to have children. However, I seem to recall Delphine had a child who may have been from a previous relationship, or else was the child of a relative killed in the war.'

With growing excitement Peter asked, 'Can you remember the child's name?'

'Yes, she was called Juliette and she used to come here when Delphine paid us visits on Pierre's behalf. I think she even came with both Delphine and Pierre on one occasion.'

'Do you by any chance know if Juliette still lives in this area?'

'No, I don't know where she is now.'

'Monsieur you have been enormously helpful, I am most grateful. By the way, am I correct in thinking you gave my uncle a present of a pair of silver candlesticks?'

'Yes, it was to thank him for a very large order. My wife and I had dinner with him and Delphine to celebrate. We had a most enjoyable evening and I remember my wife commenting that Delphine appeared to be devoted to him although I seem to recall he had not long been married.'

'Finally, may I ask if you know Delphine's married name?'

'Yes, she is now Madame Sancy.'

Peter took his leave but not before purchasing a sizeable Camembert which he hoped would still be in good condition when he got back to London. He sat in his car for a while and was uncertain how to proceed. Having been given Delphine's address and phone number he was in a quandary as to whether to telephone her or to take a chance by calling on her at her home. Eventually his decision was made because of her close proximity and his overwhelming wish to meet the woman who had played such an important part in his uncle's life both during and immediately after the war. He followed the directions he had been given and soon found himself outside an attractive half-timbered house with an adjacent barn outside in which some cows were munching contentedly. He then realised that he couldn't bring himself to simply appear at her door without an introduction, so he dialled her number. A woman's voice answered, 'Bonjour c'est Delphine'.

'Bonjour Madame. Je suis Anglais, le neveu de Pierre Vaillant. May I speak to you in English?'

'But certainly, what is it you want?'

'Sadly, Madame, my uncle died a year ago and I am trying to finalise some outstanding legal queries relating to his estate. I am anxious to talk to you about these and wondered if you could spare the time to see me?'

A few moments' silence elapsed before Delphine replied.

'I am sorry, I was taken aback by your news. I knew Pierre had been ill but we had corresponded much less often recently and I was not aware of his death. When were you wishing to see me?'

Peter took a deep breath and said, 'Madame, I have been trying to find you for some time and only established that you are still alive and where you live half an hour ago. I am calling you on a mobile phone and am sitting in my car just outside your house. Are you able to spare some time to see me now?'

Peter heard what sounded like laughter. 'You are just like your uncle. He appeared in my life completely unexpectedly and continued to do so on many occasions afterwards. Please come in, it will be a pleasure to meet you – he mentioned you to me quite often.'

AS HE WALKED towards the house, Peter wished he had thought to bring a small gift, but his misgivings were immediately dispelled when the heavy oak door opened and he was greeted with a hug by an elderly but still attractive slim woman with brown eyes and hair arranged in a chignon.

'It is a great pleasure to meet you finally,' said Peter. 'You are a very difficult person to track down.'

'I can't imagine why you say that, I have lived around here all my life.'

Peter was shown into a comfortable sitting room with a low beamed ceiling and furnished in a traditional style.

'Can I get you some refreshment?'

'Just some water would be fine.'

'Are you sure? I have just made a pot of coffee.'

'The water would be perfect just now.'

Delphine brought him a glass of water and then sat down opposite with a mug of coffee.

'Your news is a great shock – I was very fond of your uncle. But how can I be of help to you?' she said.

Peter started to explain the circumstances that had led him to try to find her and of the potential loose ends that were causing Pierre's lawyers concern. He went on to tell her how he had traced the packing cases and what they contained, as well as how he had learnt of Pierre's wartime experiences from Mark Carter and Ted Docherty's son Mike. He explained he had only the sketchiest idea of what had happened in France in 1944 and then told Delphine that he was aware she had a daughter who was also Pierre's child.

'How one's past can catch one up,' said Delphine. 'I thought I could take that secret to the grave.'

'Madame, I ...'

'Please call me Delphine.'

'Thank you, I simply wanted to say that I have no wish to intrude on your personal life or create problems for you but I am anxious to help the executors to finalise matters relating to Pierre's estate and to try to clear up some outstanding questions, particularly about your relationship with him during and after the war.'

'Of course, it is a long story. How much time do you have?'

'I am at your disposal, but I know you are married and I don't wish to disrupt any plans you may have for the day.'

'That is not a problem. My husband is away visiting a sick relative near Bayeux and will not be back until later in the week. Apart from milking the cows I am free all day. Where would you like me to start?'

'Perhaps when you first met Pierre.'

'Before telling you about my first meeting with Pierre and his role within our group I should explain the situation in our region after the fall of France. During the German Occupation of the north and west of France, our life was one long round of shortages, of food, coal, petrol, diesel fuel and of course manpower, as many of our young men were held as prisoners of war. Others were transferred to Germany against their will to work as forced labourers. We were also required to pay the cost of the German army of Occupation which imposed an unbearable burden on the economy. The lack of food led to lengthy queues at shops where the absence of meat meant that we lived mostly on potatoes, turnips and other root vegetables. Sugar ceased to exist and coffee disappeared to be replaced by a substitute made from chicory and toasted barley. Here, in the countryside, we were better off with more vegetables and cheese, but in the towns and cities life was very hard and many elderly people and young children were virtually starving. The black market was rife but the penalties if one was caught were very severe – this was the backdrop to our daily life.

'We became resourceful in adapting to these impositions by finding ways round some of the problems. Vehicles were converted to burn wood or charcoal, shoes were soled with wood and we even managed to make soap, which had completely disappeared from the shops. Our life was made even more difficult by the curfew which stopped us from going out at night unless we carried papers giving us special authorisation. As you can imagine in such an environment, hostility to the Germans became a breeding ground for various forms of resistance. Initially these took the form of strikes, demonstrations and non-cooperation, with enforced labourers doing work slowly or badly, but soon sabotage became common, as did the hiding of Jews and downed flyers. Underground publications started to appear and as the Germans cracked down, the scale and scope of activity became more militant. Small cells or units were established armed with stolen weapons and raids were undertaken on offices to steal food coupons or to destroy information about Jews.'

'May I ask how you got involved?' said Peter.

'At first it was just in carrying messages. When the Occupation began in 1940 I was still at school but this was disrupted as a result of a shortage of teachers, some of whom had been forced into labouring. Being a school girl, I was not suspected when I cycled about carrying pamphlets and other subversive material. Later I was asked to keep watch on convoys and became a lookout when raids were being undertaken. By the time I left school, I was also sending coded messages to SOE headquarters in London. In 1943, there was a forced labour draft and most of the remaining young men in our area were either taken away to Germany or went into hiding. Not long after this, I became one of a committee of three in charge of all operations in our area which comprised five adjacent villages.

'As I had learnt English at school, I was now given responsibility for liaison with London and with other cells in the Normandy region that were particularly active in helping allied airmen to escape. It was agreed I would not take part directly in attacks on bridges, railways or troop trains in case these led to a firefight, since although I could handle a revolver and a Sten gun, my colleagues felt I had more value as an English speaker liaising with London about drops of supplies or the arrival of agents in the Pays d'Auge region.'

'Is this how you initially made contact with Pierre?'

'Yes, by coded transmissions. I was in regular touch with SOE handlers as well as Free French operatives. Before Pierre and the others who accompanied him were dropped into our area, we had been warned to expect individual agents on three previous occasions. Two of them were French and were replacing regional Resistance leaders, the other was English but spoke perfect German. I understand he had been born in Germany and educated there until he was seventeen, when his parents returned to England fearing an outbreak of hostilities. He was obviously a spy and stayed with us only a few hours before leaving for Paris.'

'Tell me about the circumstances surrounding Pierre's arrival.'

'We had been alerted to plans for allied landings via coded messages over the BBC. Although we had no knowledge of where they would occur, we suspected from meaningless messages such as "the rooks will be nesting higher next month", that something was imminent. We were told to expect a number of operatives including specialist saboteurs who would work with us in coordinating activity in our area. Pierre was to stay with us and be ready to link with allied troops and facilitate contacts with other Resistance groups as they advanced. On the night of his arrival, we were briefed to expect five or six specialists who would be dropped at around midnight. German coastal defences north of us were very active and there was a considerable amount of anti-aircraft fire before the plane arrived. It appeared to be quite low as it passed over us, just before we caught sight of five parachutes silhouetted against the dark sky. They came down safely very close to each other, guided by our signals from the ground. I remember following the path of the plane which looked to be losing height rapidly as it went out of sight towards the south east.'

'Did you think it might crash?'

'I had no idea, but it seemed very much lower than previous planes had been when dropping supplies or agents. However we didn't have time to give it much thought – we quickly buried the parachutes and introductions were made. One of the group was a woman who appeared to be French and left almost immediately with a Resistance member from a village four kilometres away – I understand her role was to be similar to Pierre's but operating a little further east. Apart from Pierre, the other three were explosives and demolition experts who would be concentrating on targets which had already been identified by

London in coded messages. We split up, Pierre and another companion called Alain coming with me, whilst the other two went off with the rest of our group to a nearby village. Pierre, who appeared to be in his early twenties, had papers saying he was my cousin, and if questioned, could produce a doctor's report showing he was suffering from a severe heart condition. Alain, who was in his thirties and an explosives expert, would be staying with one of our neighbours. I seem to recall his cover story was that he had been a dock worker in Le Havre but was now unemployed as a result of allied air attacks in the dock area.

'We were soon at my parents' house and Pierre gave us a brief outline of the role he was to play and also the probable timing of the Invasion. Shortly afterwards, as it was now very late, Pierre asked if he could get to bed as he wanted some sleep before an early start in the morning. I eventually got to sleep myself, but during the night was awoken by sounds in the yard behind our barn. However, seeing nothing I went back to bed. In the morning I was told that Pierre's plane had crashed, but that the airmen had not been injured and three of them had been brought to our barn for safety. I found this rather disconcerting, so after breakfast I went to Pierre's room to tell him the news. I found him poring over maps covered in different coloured markers with symbols signifying German armour and troop deployment. He told me he was anxious to meet with as many of the local Resistance leaders as possible in order to try to verify the data on the maps. We agreed I should arrange a meeting later in the day and he then went over to the barn to check on the airmen as apparently two of them were good friends of his. We then both went off to our meeting.'

Delphine broke off to get herself another cup of coffee. She persuaded Peter to join her and also to sample a piece of home-made apple cake.

'That is absolutely delicious,' said Peter.

'It's my speciality, although there are many different variations. Apples are abundant here so we use them in many of our desserts. Your uncle was particularly fond of my recipe!'

'I can well imagine why. You were just saying that you met up with other Resistance leaders.'

'Yes, we met in the crypt of a nearby church with lookouts carefully stationed to keep an eye open for Germans. There were nearly twenty people present, each of whom could probably mobilise a dozen or more others. Pierre talked in considerable detail about plans for the Invasion but did not reveal the exact date nor the place where Allied forces would land. He did, however, spell out exactly what he wanted our groups to do and then said he would like to have individual sessions with each of the leaders, for reasons of security. At that point I left and he told me to expect him back in our village the next morning. When I got back I went over to the barn to see how the flyers were getting on. They complained a great deal about not being able to smoke but cheered up when I said we would try to get them away and en route to Spain within a day or two.

'The following morning Pierre appeared quite early. He looked very tired but was pleased with the way things had gone in his meetings. A number of detailed and complex plans had apparently been discussed, particularly those aimed at the enemy's communications. I had a sense that what he called D-Day was now imminent. He told me he was anxious to get the Americans away so there could be no danger of them being captured and jeopardising our plans. He felt this was so important that he asked me to arrange for them to be put into the pipeline to Spain that night and to go with them on the first leg to ensure they were well away from our area. A little later, after I had made the arrangements, we both went over to the barn to tell them the plan and warn them to be ready to leave with me in the evening.

'As the day wore on, I sensed that Pierre was almost as anxious about my task as he had been about his own the previous day. He told me to be especially careful and not to take chances en route and gave me his own revolver just in case I found myself in real trouble. Having acted as a courier in accompanying downed pilots on a number of previous occasions I was amused by his concern, but thought he was very sweet to be so caring!

'As soon as it was dark, Pierre came to say goodbye to his friends and he gave me a big hug before wishing us all a safe journey. I was joined by two members of my group who were well armed in case we encountered any German patrols. We moved fast, sticking to wooded areas where possible and avoiding open ground. On a couple of occasions we had to stop for a short time as we heard the sound of military vehicles but despite the fact that the Americans were not used to hiking over rough ground we made good progress. I was anxious about getting them under cover before daybreak and kept pushing on, but even with delays we arrived at our destination in good time having covered nearly thirty kilometres. We had a quick breakfast together and I slept for a couple of hours but, before leaving, I gave them some cigarettes and wished them a safe journey to the Spanish border. After the war, I heard they had made it back to England and that their squadron had subsequently been posted to France where apparently they met up again with Pierre.

'I spent a lot of time with Pierre in the next few of days reconnoitring railway lines, bridges and German tank positions which I then radioed back to London. Your uncle was a charming, kind and thoughtful man, always concerned about the risks I was taking and very appreciative of what I was doing to help him. I pointed out that I was doing it for France but he invariably expressed admiration for what he described as my courage and commitment. One night we were nearly caught by a German patrol who spotted us checking the controls of a signal box on the line between Caen and Mézidon. We exchanged fire but managed to get away, as I knew the way to a deserted barn where we buried ourselves in the bales of hay. We lay there for a long time listening for any sound that might have indicated we were being followed. Eventually we fell asleep.

'When I woke I found that Pierre had taken off his jacket and put it over me but was now pressed very tightly against me to keep warm. After a while he stirred slightly, opened his eyes and kissed me gently first on the cheek and then on my lips. I responded and very soon our mutual affection gave way to passionate lovemaking. At that moment I realised I was falling in love with Pierre and I thought he felt the same about me. However we had to restrain our emotions from further expression as we were still in potential danger. Shortly afterwards I whispered to Pierre that I was going to take a look outside. Everything was quiet so we slipped away and were back safely home without encountering any more obstacles.'

'Did this change in your relationship create any problems in tackling your planned assignments?'

'Not really, although I sensed that Pierre was even more protective than previously and he seemed especially concerned when I was away at night. He often tried to accompany me but this was not always practical. At about this time, signals traffic from London increased considerably and then we received a message "the fox is approaching the hen coup" which Pierre now told me was the code for the launch of the Invasion. In the next twenty-four hours he threw himself into a frantic whirlwind of meetings, always with his map as a planning aid. He had organised a number of acts of sabotage on railways and bridges for the night of June 5, all of which were coordinated to slow down troop transports going north to the coast. I urged him to rest but apart from coming to my room briefly for a couple of hours during the night he pushed himself to the limit, saying he could not spare the time until our objectives were completed. The following morning, news bulletin reported that the Allies had landed along a stretch of coast north west of Caen – at last we sensed that liberation was near!'

'How did you react to this long awaited news?'

'We were elated but it was probably the time of our greatest danger. There were constant German troop movements with tanks and heavy artillery everywhere. We had been requested to maintain continuous attacks on strategic positions which were increasingly well guarded, but through a combination of diversionary tactics and the immense courage shown by some of our compatriots, efforts to slow down enemy reinforcements were proving to be effective. However, Pierre was finding it increasingly difficult to move around as German troops were everywhere. He relied on me more and more to help him to find secure routes to reach other teams and to coordinate activity. I found I was spending all my time with him and as a result our feelings for each other intensified, even though there were limited opportunities to express them. We were now attacking trains nightly in order to slow down the progress of men and armaments to the front and our efforts were becoming more and more reckless.

'One morning, about ten days after D-Day, I was driving with Alain and two other demolition specialists through some quiet roads near our village. The boot of the car was full of dynamite and fuses and we knew we were taking a risk but we stupidly believed we would not run into any trouble. We suddenly found ourselves confronted by a roadblock manned by four Germans with machine guns. One came over to ask for our papers. At first everything seemed to be in order but he then asked to see in the boot. Alain drew a gun and shot him and told me to make a run for it. I accelerated towards the roadblock and was through it when machine gun fire punctured two of the tyres. I jumped out and started running away. The others engaged the Germans with their guns but they were no match for the machine gun and were quickly wounded. At that point, two of the Germans came after me and, as I was unarmed, I had to surrender. I was thrown into the back of a truck together with my colleagues, one of whom was dead. Alain was wounded in the shoulder, but he whispered to me that I should say I had been forced at gunpoint to drive the car and that he would confirm my story. We were taken to the local headquarters where interrogation commenced.'

'Delphine, I feel you must be finding this all very wearing. Would you like to stop and continue another time?'

'I am happy to go on but I would like to have some lunch. Would you care to join me in something simple – perhaps a little cheese, some bread and a glass of wine?'

'If it wouldn't be too much trouble some lunch would be most welcome, but I'm a little concerned that bringing back the past may be reawakening painful memories.'

'I am fine but, while we eat, tell me a little about yourself Peter. Is your mother still alive?'

'No, sadly both my parents are now dead. I was married for a while but now live alone in a flat in central London. I used to be a director of a public relations company but for the last three years I've been semi-retired, although I still have one or two clients to whom I give advice on strategy and marketing. I seem to manage fairly well on my own although I do find that time can occasionally drag when I'm not fully occupied. When Pierre died I must confess I hadn't expected there to be many complications in tying up his estate, but having found out about a hitherto unknown part of his life, I need to clarify a few things for the lawyers before they can close their files.'

Delphine had put cheese, bread and fruit on the table and asked Peter to open a bottle of wine.

'It's a local wine we drink a little like water – I hope it's acceptable. Please help yourself.'

'It's excellent Delphine, thank you so much for your kindness and for sparing me so much of your time.'

'Peter, if you don't mind I would prefer not to go back over the details of that terrible period following my capture, interrogation and eventual internment. It was a nightmare of fear, brutality, hunger, cold, desperation and hopelessness. The only thing that kept me sane was that I found I was pregnant and was carrying Pierre's child. This gave me the will to live and I knew in my heart that salvation would eventually come. I tried smuggling letters out of the camp but had no idea whether they reached him or whether he was still alive. I prayed for him and me and our unborn child and most of all that we would be reunited when the war ended.

'Autumn gave way to winter and the weather was appalling with heavy snowfall – the cold was intense and we all suffered through lack of food. One of the guards, seeing my condition, took pity on me and gave me a little extra food and also some chocolate saying I needed food for two! Just after Christmas two new inmates appeared and told us that a huge battle was taking place near Falaise and that the enemy was being pushed back towards Germany. We all greeted 1945 with high hopes that the war would end very soon and, about three weeks later, we awoke one morning to find that the guards had fled. We were free at last!

'It's difficult for me to put into words how we all felt that morning. We were still cold and hungry but also elated in believing the worst was now over and we would soon be able to get home to those we loved. The next day a couple of American jeeps which were reconnoitring the area appeared, and very soon afterwards a large contingent of very tired, dirty but cheerful troops. Their priority was to get some sleep but before doing so they gave us food and warmer clothing. We looked like a bunch of half starved tramps, but they treated us with great respect and genuine warmth and restored our faith in humanity. We asked whether it was safe to leave the camp and were told by their commanding officer that the road to Paris was reasonably clear as the city had been liberated four months earlier. He warned us about small groups of Germans who had become separated from their units but said there were refugee groups going in both directions and if we stuck to the main roads we should be safe.

'I left the next day with two other women who came from the same area as me. We managed to get lifts some of the way to Paris, where I contacted a friend who gave me the money for the train fare to Caen. I stayed there overnight and was home the following morning. As you can imagine, my family were overjoyed to see me but were alarmed to see that I was pregnant. However, when I explained that the child was Pierre's they calmed down a little. They told me he had been gone for some time and they believed he had been moved to work on projects in Caen. My father asked me whether Pierre knew that the baby was his and that it was imminent. He was particularly concerned about whether I had heard from him. When I told my father I had written and entrusted the letter to a good friend, but there had been no reply, he made me write again to the Free French HQ in London, as he could not believe Pierre would have ignored my previous letter had he received it. More time passed and I was feeling very much stronger, but I was still distressed to have heard nothing from Pierre. None of the radio contacts I had made in London seemed to be accessible and I began to wonder whether Pierre had abandoned me.

'Meanwhile my mother was helping me with plans for the baby's arrival. We managed to buy a few essential items and she and an aunt were busy knitting, using wool they had obtained via black market sources. In the second week of March our daughter, Juliette, was born. She was a lovely, happy little girl with Pierre's eyes and a cute little nose. My mother and I doted on her, but as soon as I felt able I knew I had to get a job. My mother agreed to look after Juliette and I went to work as a receptionist at a nearby hotel in Monteille. I had a photograph taken of me with Juliette and wrote again to Pierre enclosing the picture. I gave the letter to a Free French officer who was attending a conference in London and was convinced he would be able to locate him, so I felt optimistic I would hear something before too long.'

'I found all three letters in a packing case in England, so obviously they did reach him eventually,' said Peter.

'Yes, I heard much later he had received them, but unfortunately not until long after Juliette was born and tragically by that time he was married.'

'Do you have any idea why he didn't get them sooner?'

'I don't know, but Pierre told me that my last letter came first and that was not until May! Apparently the other two arrived together about a month later, having been forwarded from London to Caen, by which time he had left there. I subsequently learnt that the Free French HQ in London had been virtually disbanded in August 1944, when Paris was liberated and de

Gaulle came back to France, so their administration in London had been reduced to no more than a skeleton staff.'

'When did you hear from him finally?'

'He wrote as soon as he received the letter with the photograph. He was immensely relieved to hear I had survived internment, as he had not received any news about me despite trying to get information about where I had been taken. My pregnancy obviously came as a real shock to him, particularly as he was now married, but I think he was secretly rather excited to know that he had a baby daughter. As you can imagine, I was very distressed to learn he was married but I realised that without any news of me he must have assumed I was dead. He said he would make arrangements for me to receive money via his bank and that he would try to visit me as soon as possible. He thought it best that I write in future to the address of his American friend Ted Docherty, who was one of the three American flyers I helped when their plane crashed and who had apparently got back safely to England. Shortly afterwards, I had another letter from him enquiring about the possibility of contacting me by phone and I suggested he try ringing me at the hotel where I was working.

'A few days later he called. It was such a surprise and I was so happy to be able to talk to him after such a long time, especially as I had often despaired of ever hearing from him again. We talked about my internment, how things were in France and how I was coping with both Juliette and a job, and of course the fact that he was now married.

'He told me he was planning to come to France to explore business opportunities and said he hoped to be here in the autumn, by which time Juliette would be six months old. He phoned me again a couple of weeks later and confirmed he intended to come here in early September, when meetings had been arranged with cheese makers with whom he was planning to do business. He enquired about staying at the hotel where I worked and asked if I could reserve a room for him for three nights. After that he called me quite frequently and he always enquired about Juliette. I found it very difficult to come to terms with his marriage but I recognised that war had devastated many people's lives and I took comfort from the fact that we had both survived and we had such a lovely baby.

'When the time came for his visit I was so excited the manager reprimanded me for neglecting some of my duties, but I think he understood the reason and was not too hard on me since I was finally going to be reunited with Juliette's father.'

Delphine stopped and looked up at the clock.

'Oh dear, I am sorry but I have been talking for such a long time and I must get on with milking the cows. I do hope I have been able to give you all the information you needed, but if there are other questions, perhaps we could meet again.'

'Of course, I feel I have imposed on you far too long already, but there are some other things I wanted to talk to you about and I would like to know more about Juliette. Is it possible for you to spare a little more time tomorrow? I'm staying in Caen and it wouldn't take me long to get back here.'

'That is not necessary, I could meet you in Caen. I go there quite often to shop but would need to get back here by around three o'clock to deal with cows.'

'Well if it's not too much trouble, I'd be most grateful. Would you like to come at around 10.30 and, if you have time, perhaps you would join me for an early lunch before returning?'

'That would be most enjoyable, 10.30 would suit me fine.'

Peter gave Delphine the address of his hotel and left with another piece of the apple cake she insisted he should take with him. When he got back in his hotel he decided to visit the silversmith to buy a gift for her. However, before doing so, he called Richard Anstruther's office. His secretary put Peter straight through.

'Richard, I've met Delphine and now understand much more about her relationship with Pierre, how she became pregnant and why Pierre didn't know about Juliette until after he was married. It's a very long story and I didn't get a chance to ask her what she meant by the "package" to which she referred in one of her letters, nor to find out whether she knew anything about Pierre having an account with BNP.'

'Peter, have you not listened to the message I left on your mobile earlier?'

'I'm sorry, I left it in the car when I called on Delphine, is it something important?'

'I think that might be a slight understatement. In going through the files we've now come across a document which reveals that Pierre secretly adopted Juliette as his daughter in 1966.'

'Good Lord, that's extraordinary. I can hardly believe it – it seems there's no end to the surprises in his past! This presumably means there could be a number of major implications in finalising the legal matters that are still outstanding?'

'To be perfectly honest, Peter, I'm not completely sure how it'll affect the situation. However, I'll certainly have to discuss this with the French lawyers as I think there'll be important issues relating to dependent's rights of inheritance which could affect a number of those named in his Will, particularly you and Mme Martin, since you are currently the main beneficiaries from the estate.'

'Is that because under Continental law the child or children of a deceased person have a prior claim over a person's assets?'

'Broadly, yes but there may be other issues as well, such as the possibility of obligations to Delphine, now you've located her. I'm going to ask for the translation of the contents of the files to be given much higher priority and in the meantime, now you're in the picture, I'll be briefing my opposite number in Nice – in confidence, of course.'

'Should I mention I know about this to Delphine?'

'I don't see why not as she must aware of it. I can't believe for a moment Pierre would have adopted Juliette without discussing his plans with her.'

'Well, Richard, this is certainly proving to be much more complicated than being asked if I could sort out a few loose ends. I hope there aren't going to be any more unforeseen surprises!'

'I couldn't agree more, but in the meantime we'll press on with the translation of the rest of the files as quickly as possible – and please keep your mobile with you as we may need to talk again!'

CHAPTER SEVEN

PETER DECIDED HE needed a drink to help him relax before
doing anything else. He went to the bar, ordered a whisky and
sunk himself in a comfortable armchair. Richard was right: the
implications of this latest revelation were considerable not only
for him but particularly for Helene Martin, who had clearly been
hoping that the estate would be worth rather more once the
mystery of the contents of the packing cases had been resolved.
He realised his own legacy would be affected, but now he
had found out so much about Delphine and Juliette he felt
comfortable with Richard's revelation. When he saw Delphine
the following day he resolved to press her for more information
about Pierre's relationship with her and Juliette after the war.
Finishing his drink he paid another visit to the silversmith, where
he thanked the assistant again for his help in identifying the
purchaser of the candlesticks and then bought a silver cake knife
as a present for Delphine.

Once he was back in his room, Peter rang room service to
order an omelette with an accompanying mixed salad and half a
bottle of wine. As he ate he made a few notes about the points
he wanted to be sure to cover with Delphine the following
morning. He found himself constantly thinking about Juliette's
adoption by his uncle and he wondered if anyone other than
Delphine, who he assumed must have agreed to it, was aware of
his uncle's decision. He was about to go to bed when his phone
rang. It was Suzanne.

'Hello Peter, I hope it's not too late to call but I gather from Maman that there's a new development.'

'What makes you say that?'

'She was talking to Maître Simon, and got the impression there could be some major complications. She appears to be quite agitated, largely as he wouldn't tell her any details or how it could affect her personally.'

'I can't tell you anything as it's all about legal issues. All being well they should be resolved reasonably quickly.'

'That'll be a relief. When are you coming back to Nice?'

'Probably when everything is finalised, which I'm hoping will be quite soon.'

'Let me know when you'll be here, it would be really good to see you again.'

'I will, of course. How are things with you?'

'I'm fine but I do wish everything was finalised – Maman's preoccupation with her potential legacy is really getting to me.'

'Well let's hope for all our sakes that it gets finalised soon. I'll give you a call when I'm coming back.'

'That would be lovely; I look forward to seeing you again.'

'Me too, take care.'

Peter put down the phone and couldn't help feeling annoyed by the conversation, even though he was pleased to have heard from Suzanne. He was surprised to hear that Helene Martin already had some inkling there could be complications and he realised she was going to be flabbergasted once she heard about Juliette. 'Thank goodness it's not my problem,' he thought before getting to bed.

He slept badly, turning Richard's call over and over in his mind. Once up he decided to go for a long walk, which helped to clear his head, and he returned to the hotel feeling very much better. After a croissant and a couple of cups of excellent coffee he went up to his room to take a quick look at the notes he had made in readiness for the meeting with Delphine. Shortly afterwards, reception called to tell him he had a visitor. He hurried down and greeted her.

'It's great to see you again, Delphine, and thank you so much for sparing more time for me. I have a small gift to thank you for your kindness yesterday – I hope you'll find it acceptable.'

'How very kind Peter, shall I open it now?'

'Maybe you'd like to open it later – why don't we find a quiet corner in the lounge?'

Once they had settled, Peter ordered some coffee.

'Delphine, do you mind if I ask you about what happened after you were reunited with Pierre, and also more about Juliette?'

'Of course not but, as you will appreciate, it's quite a long story. Where would you like me to start?'

'Perhaps when Pierre visited you for the first time.'

'Well, as I mentioned yesterday, Pierre planned to combine his visit around meetings with cheese manufacturers whose products he was hoping to import to England. He arrived in September the year Juliette was born and, as you can imagine, I was immensely excited at the prospect of seeing him after more than a year. When we met we were both a little awkward with each other, but when he saw Juliette he became much more relaxed, just as I had remembered him. He explained he had been unable to trace me after I was captured despite his various efforts, and had finally gone ahead with his marriage as he had been engaged before coming to France the previous year.'

'How did he react to having a daughter?'

'He was thrilled, although he realised she created a big problem for me and especially my mother, who had to look after her whilst I was at work. He said he would make a proper arrangement for Juliette to be provided for and suggested that, if he could develop some business locally, perhaps I could assist him with it. While he was here the three of us spent as much time as we could together and we went into Lisieux to buy Juliette some toys and baby clothes. I was so happy to see him but obviously sad that he had to go so quickly, although he promised to ring regularly and come to see us again as soon as he could.'

'When did you see him next?'

'I had been awarded the Médaille de la Résistance early in 1946 in recognition of my efforts against the enemy. He called me not long after and told me he had been invited to come to France to receive the same medal and another being awarded to SOE operatives. We both went to Paris and had a wonderful weekend visiting galleries, museums and the Opera, but as usual it was over too soon.'

'And was he able to see Juliette growing up?'

'For a number of years he was here at least once a year and sometimes more often. We had agreed that in view of our complicated circumstances, Pierre would be known as "Uncle Pierre" to Juliette, and she was led to believe her father had died in the war. As she grew older she used to ask more and more frequently about her uncle and when she would next be seeing him. He wrote to her often and sent her Christmas and birthday presents, while she sent him cards from the places we visited on holiday, although I was very unhappy about the unreal way we were living.'

'Did the three of you ever go on holiday together?'

'Only for a weekend during one of Pierre's short visits. We went to Deauville and stayed at a delightful hotel overlooking the beach. I think Juliette was fourteen and starting to be more grown-up. She loved it and said to me "Can't Uncle Pierre come and stay with us more often so that we can do this again?" We were both very sad about our situation and I think Pierre felt especially bad, as from then on he came to see us rather less frequently. He still phoned and wrote but I think he had a bad conscience.'

'That must have been very painful, how did it affect your relationship?'

'Over the years, I had helped a great deal with his business contacts and he was very generous financially, but both Juliette and I felt a huge void in our lives. I had always received a great deal of attention from men but had shown little interest in them. However, when Juliette was eighteen, I received a marriage proposal which I decided to accept and was married two years later. Maurice is a kind and caring man and he was fond of Juliette so it seemed the right thing to do. Needless to say, although Pierre was happy for me, I think he was disappointed, since he knew it would obviously change our relationship, which I suppose was inevitable.'

'I understand Pierre adopted Juliette in secret in 1966. Is this something you had discussed in the past or was it a sudden decision?'

'Pierre had talked about it from time to time as I think he was anxious she should benefit from his estate when he died. When Juliette was eighteen she went to university but dropped out after her first year. She seemed very unsettled and I think she may have taken drugs. She worked for a while in publishing but never seemed to settle for long. Although, as I said, Maurice was very kind, she didn't seem to be comfortable here in Normandy and I didn't see her as often as I would have liked. However, she had her own life to lead and she had a number of different boyfriends; some I met and quite liked, others were a disaster. I used to worry a lot about her and probably rang Pierre with my concerns more than I should. He seemed very philosophical about it, reminding me of how I had been when he met me at roughly the same age. That did not make me feel any better but I think it finally led to the decision that he would like to adopt her. It was handled by lawyers here in France and he asked me to be discreet about it for obvious reasons, as he did not want his wife to know about his past.'

'How did Juliette feel when she heard the news?'

'I think she was secretly rather pleased, although she was now twenty and quite an independent young woman. She would probably have been more excited if it had happened a few years earlier but Pierre made a great fuss of the occasion. He arranged for it to be formalised just before her twenty-first birthday to coincide with a visit to one of his big local suppliers. We went to a lovely restaurant beside the River Orne in Caen which Pierre said had special memories for him. He was in great spirits, we had lots of champagne and I think Juliette felt very special, particularly when Pierre told her how much he loved her and that he wanted her to feel she was very important to him, even though he lived in England and it would have to remain a secret. She asked about visiting him in England and he explained that it might be difficult because he did not have an easy relationship with his wife, but that she could come to London at any time and he would show her around the various places of interest. She asked if I could come too – to my delight he said "of course".'

At this point one of the waiters came over to enquire whether they wanted anything more.

'Would you like another coffee or perhaps a glass of wine?' enquired Peter.

'A glass of Chablis would be lovely and, as I shall have to leave in an hour or so, maybe I could have a sandwich to accompany it.'

Peter ordered sandwiches for them both and, while he was waiting, mentioned that he had bought Delphine's present from a silversmith who had helped him to trace her. She opened the wrapping and immediately recognised the name on the box.

'I know this shop – Pierre was given a pair of candlesticks from Vigneux as a present by one of his big suppliers and they told him he could change them if they were not to his taste. I seem to remember he was very fond of them as a memento of his business dealings here. Peter, this is lovely, what a wonderful present and how very kind of you. I shall be able to use it to serve my apple cake next time you come to see me!'

'I'm glad you like it and I look forward to the next occasion, which I hope is very soon. As you'll have to leave shortly I did want to ask you a couple of other things that might be relevant to the issues that are concerning the lawyers. I wonder, do you recall whether Pierre had an account with Banque Nationale de Paris?'

'Why yes, Pierre had accounts with two or three banks which he used to finance his export deals. I think his main account was with Crédit Agricole but he certainly had an account with BNP, which I believe is now BNP Paribas.'

'You don't remember where he had the account by any chance?'

'I think he may have opened it in London but I believe he also used to have dealings with one of their people at the branch here in Rue de Vaucelles. Of course, that was many years ago.'

'Perhaps I'll give them a call later to see whether they can help. Delphine, may I ask you a little more about Juliette as she will now be a beneficiary from Pierre's estate? But, before that, I wonder if I could jog your memory about something you mentioned to Pierre in one of your letters after you got out of the internment camp. You made reference to a package being hidden – is this something you can tell me more about and might it be of significance in tying up the loose ends of his estate?'

For a moment Delphine was taken aback by the question, but she quickly recovered her composure.

'Peter, I hope you will understand that a great deal of my relationship with Pierre was inevitably a secret between us because of our unusual circumstances. Until now I have not discussed with anyone what I have told you, nor would I have done, but now Pierre is dead it doesn't matter. There are many things from the past that will have to remain a secret because they are nobody else's business but ours. I have been happy to try to answer your questions, as I am anxious to be helpful and I hope that in doing so it may ultimately be of benefit to Juliette who, I suspect, has suffered a great deal in not having a father. What you have asked me relates to something Pierre chose to keep to himself and never divulged to me, although I do know something about it. For that reason I find it difficult to discuss it with you.'

'Delphine, I do understand, if this was something very personal between you. However, I was hoping you might be able to tell me what it related to, especially if it has any bearing on his estate.'

'I really don't feel able to talk about something which is really none of my business, I'm sorry.'

'No, I'm in the wrong, I shouldn't have bothered you about it. Please forgive me, I'm sure it's not important. Perhaps you would care for another glass of wine?'

'I won't have another glass of wine, but some coffee would be most welcome.'

Peter ordered coffee for both of them and also asked for the bill.

'I'd very much like to meet Juliette. Does she live locally?'

'No she has a flat in Paris and lives alone. She has had a number of affairs but never felt she wanted to settle down. Let me give you her phone number.'

'You don't think she would object to me contacting her?'

'I'm sure she would be happy to meet someone who is part of Pierre's family. However, although their relationship had not been quite so close in recent years, I am sure she will be distressed to hear of his death. If you don't mind I would like to break the news to her before you call.'

'Of course. Maybe you would let me know when it would be appropriate for me to call her. There's just one other thing I'd like to clarify in view of the fact that the life you shared with Pierre has only just emerged. Were you receiving any financial support from him up until the time he died and, if so, might I ask where it came from?'

'Pierre made arrangements for me to receive financial assistance whilst Juliette was growing up and he bought me a little car when I was helping him with his business dealings so I could visit his contacts. He also gave me the money to enable me to buy the house where I am living with Maurice and it is still in my name. However, he stopped paying the allowance once Juliette was twenty-one. He may have an arrangement with her but I know nothing about that.'

'Well that helps to clarify something which had been puzzling me. As the financial arrangements had been discontinued, that explains why there was no record of your existence until I came across the papers in Mike Docherty's barn.'

'You may be right Peter, but I suspect it's also because Pierre was at heart both ashamed and embarrassed about what happened in his past and took extreme steps to cover his tracks. But he was a good and generous man and the events of those days in the summer of 1944 were both unplanned and unexpected and, of course, we were both young and living for the moment. I do not regret anything that occurred, although I feel Juliette may have suffered more than I realise. But I must go now if you will excuse me, as I must get back to my cows before they become restless.'

'I'm so grateful for your candour, Delphine, and for sharing what must, at times, have been a painful recollection of the past. I'm sure you realise how sorry I am to have been the person to have brought you the news of Pierre's death, even though it occurred last year. Once everything is resolved I'll let you know and, as I mentioned, now we know Juliette was his daughter it'll have a considerable bearing on the final disposition of his estate.'

'Peter, please don't trouble yourself. What we have talked about took place such a long time ago it was difficult at times to recall it. I have so enjoyed meeting you and look forward to hearing from you again very soon.'

Peter went with her to the door and watched her walking away. 'What an extraordinary and unusually independent woman,' he thought. 'She must have been remarkable when Pierre met her all those years ago.'

As soon as he was back in his room Peter called Richard Anstruther, who was in a meeting and apparently unlikely to be free for at least an hour.

'Would you mind getting him to call me back?' he asked Richard's secretary.

He stood in front of his window looking across the garden and pondered what he should do as a result of his conversation with Delphine. It was clear he had to talk to Juliette and possibly even meet her and he needed to check whether the key he'd found meant Pierre had a safe deposit with BNP Paribas. He was still mystified about Delphine's reaction to his query about the package referred to in her letter. Was she covering up something she didn't want to disclose or did she merely not know anything more about it? He found it very perplexing but, in the meantime, he rang reception to arrange to stay another night in Caen.

Shortly afterwards Richard called.

'Sorry I missed you. How are things progressing?'

'I spent most of the morning with Delphine. We talked about Juliette and her adoption by Pierre – apparently she now lives in Paris and, as far as Delphine is aware, she doesn't know Pierre is dead. She claims he lost contact with them both in the last year or so, which I found a bit surprising. And the reason there appears to be no record of Delphine among his papers is because Pierre stopped his financial support for her when Juliette became twenty-one. I understand he gave Delphine money to buy the house she now lives in, presumably as a means of ending his financial support. By the way, I can't remember whether I told you I'd found a key with the initials "BNP" in the packing cases. Delphine confirmed that Pierre used to have an account with what is now BNP Paribas here in Caen and she thought he might have one in Paris. I'm planning to go over to the local branch but they obviously won't tell me anything without authorisation. Would you mind emailing them to introduce me and explain that I'm helping you to tie up Pierre's affairs?'

'Certainly, I'll ask my secretary to organise something right away. Is there anything else of interest?'

'I found she was rather mysterious when I asked her about the package referred to in one of her letters to Pierre. I couldn't tell whether she was trying to hide something or maybe, as she claimed, he never divulged to her what was in the mysterious package. Either way, I'm no closer to finding out about it at present. I do feel I have to meet Juliette to see if there is anything more to be discovered about Pierre's past and what arrangements he may have secretly made for her support. So I plan to stay here one more day and then drive back tomorrow. Meanwhile, how are you getting on with translating the files?'

'My colleague is still working on them when she can find the time – I hope to have more news for you when you get back to London.'

'Thanks Richard. Would you mind letting me have a copy of your email to the bank so I can produce it if required.'

'Certainly, it should be with you in about fifteen minutes.'

Peter took a look at his map and found that the bank was reasonably close to the hotel, so he decided to walk rather than take his car. He waited a quarter of an hour and then went to reception to enquire about his email. A few minutes later, the concierge brought it over and he set off. Arriving at the bank, he asked for the foreign department and, having shown his email, was asked to take a seat in a tiny waiting room which had sufficient space for a table and two chairs but virtually nothing else. A couple of minutes later he was joined by a young man holding the email.

'Good afternoon Monsieur Barton, my name is Guy Brissard. We have just received a copy of this email from your solicitor in London, how can we help you?'

'Thank you for seeing me at such short notice. As my solicitor has explained, I am trying to finalise some matters relating to my late uncle's estate and, having found this key with the bank's name on it, I am trying to establish whether he has a safe deposit box here in Caen.'

Peter passed the key across the table.

'This key was obviously issued after BNP was created by a merger in 1966, but before a later merger with Paribas in 2000. However, it does not look to me as though it is the key to any of our deposit boxes.'

Brissard spoke briefly to someone on the phone and a few moments later a clerk came into the room. He was instructed to check whether the key fitted any of the bank's boxes and to call back.

'While your colleague checks the key are you able to tell me if M. Vaillant still has an account with you?'

'I checked this before you came. He no longer has an account at this branch but it appears from our records that he might have one with our branch at King William Street in the City of London. I regret I am not at liberty to disclose any details to you – it would be necessary to contact them direct.'

The phone rang and, after a brief conversation, Brissard confirmed that the key was not one issued by their branch.

'Perhaps it was issued to him by our branch in the City – I am sorry I cannot be of more assistance.'

Peter took his leave and strolled back to his hotel enjoying the late afternoon sunshine which, once again, had brought crowds to the park. He caught sight of a couple with a small girl who they were swinging between them as they walked and wondered if Pierre and Delphine had ever visited this park with Juliette.

When Peter got back to the hotel he was given a message asking him to call Delphine Sancy. He had a quick glass of Calvados in the bar and then went up to his room to return her call.

'Hello Delphine, I'm sorry I missed you.'

'I was just ringing to let you know I have spoken to Juliette and told her about Pierre's death. She was very upset by the news, particularly because she had not heard from him for more than two years. Apparently they used to correspond quite regularly until about three years ago and then his letters became less and less frequent. She also had the impression that her letters were not reaching him either. He didn't have a mobile phone and, when she did try calling, she found the service had been discontinued. Seemingly, after he sold his business to his partner, he moved into a nearby lodge and became a bit of a recluse, so she thought that might be the reason As I think I mentioned, I rather lost touch with him over the years, especially after I married Maurice, so sadly neither she nor I knew of his death, which has made it all the more painful. I must confess the news has taken a little while to sink in and I am feeling a real sense of loss for someone who was a very important part of my life when I was younger. However, I am sure Juliette would be happy to talk to you if you would like to give her a call, but it would be best if you leave it till tomorrow as I think she needs a little time to come to terms with what was inevitably something of a shock.'

'Of course, I can leave it for a while if you feel that would be best. There is no urgency.'

'I don't think that would be necessary, she just needs to let the news to sink in. I am sure that if you wished to call tomorrow it would be fine.'

'I must confess, Delphine, that now I know about what happened in the past, I'm a little surprised that neither you nor Juliette were made aware of Pierre's death. I would have expected that his business partner, Hubert Young, or his mistress,

Helene Martin, would have known about you and Juliette and would have been in touch.'

'I don't know either of them, although I suppose Pierre may have mentioned me to them at some stage. From what you say it seems they are as much in the dark about Pierre's distant past as you and I are about more recent events.'

'You may be right,' said Peter. 'But I still find it curious that nobody ever mentioned Juliette to me, unless Pierre kept her adoption a complete secret from everyone.'

'Well it would seem so – will you let me know in due course if there are any more developments, and do please give my best wishes to Mark whenever you are speaking to him.'

'I certainly will Delphine, and once again my thanks for everything.'

Peter found the situation very perplexing. It was perhaps not a surprise that Delphine knew so little about Pierre's recent life if, after her marriage, she had gradually lost touch. What he found more difficult to understand was that Juliette, who had obviously tried to maintain contact, albeit infrequently and seemingly only by correspondence, had not heard of Pierre's death. He recalled that Hubert had not been particularly helpful when he was trying to find out more about the packing cases at Berwick St James and wondered if he knew more than he had revealed and, if so, what his reasons were.

Peter decided he would talk to Juliette as soon as he was back in London.

He checked out of the hotel early the following morning and was in Cherbourg in time to catch a mid-morning ferry. Although there was a light breeze, the crossing was reasonably smooth and he took the opportunity to catch up on the sports news and also the latest score in the test match against Australia. He had a late lunch in the bar before landing in Portsmouth just after three and was back in his flat in time to see the last half hour of the match and England go 2-1 up in the series.

CHAPTER EIGHT

THE NEXT MORNING Peter decided to go to a local patisserie for coffee and a croissant. As usual, it was crowded with customers having a quick snack before work, as well as others who seemed to have plenty of time to read the morning papers. He sat deep in thought, wondering whether to call Juliette or leave it for another day or two. He was also unsure what he should do to try to resolve the mystery of the key marked BNP.

After a second coffee, he decided his priority was to pay a visit to the bank in King William Street but, before doing so, he called his solicitor to arrange another letter of introduction. Richard Anstruther's secretary was happy to organise this and, as previously, to email a copy to him. He asked her to let Richard know he was back in England and would ring him later in the day.

Returning to his flat, he dealt with most of the messages on his answerphone but decided not to return a call from Mark, who had phoned two days previously, as he knew it would be a long conversation if he told him about his meeting with Delphine.

Once he had received his copy of the email to BNP Paribas, he picked up a cab to take him to King William Street. The journey to the City was like a tourist's guide to London's landmarks. Up to Hyde Park Corner, past Buckingham Palace and alongside St James's Park to Parliament Square and the Houses of Parliament, then on to the Embankment past the Eye and towards the City, where St Paul's still commanded the skyline amidst the backdrop of assorted skyscrapers. Passing the Mansion House, the cab turned in front of the Bank of England and pulled up outside the bank's London headquarters.

Having explained the purpose of his visit at reception and shown the email, he was asked to wait for a few minutes while an executive from the bank's security deposit facilities department was summoned to see him. After a short wait a young woman entered the room and introduced herself as Jane Fernley.

'I've received an email of introduction from your solicitor, would you mind letting me see some identification?'

Peter smiled, reflecting on the British obsession with security, although he fully appreciated the reason for it.

'Would a driving licence and credit card suffice?'

'Thank you, that's fine. I understand you wish to establish whether M. Vaillant has an account and a safe deposit facility here.'

'Yes, I came across this key with the bank's initials on it among some of his personal possessions. The lawyers handling his estate are anxious to establish whether there are any other assets that need to be accounted for. As I believe Mr Vaillant may have an account here, I'm trying to find out whether there is anything of value that has not yet been identified.'

Jane Fernley took the key and turned it over in her hand.

'It looks like one of our old keys. We moved into this office in 1975 and I suspect it dates from the 1970s. I'll check whether we are holding anything on his behalf but you'll appreciate that if we are, I wouldn't be able to release anything from one of our boxes without a more formal authorisation from the lawyer handling the probate.'

'I understand, but it would be most helpful if you could tell me if this is the key to a box containing items belonging to M. Vaillant and also whether anything is still lodged in it.'

'I can certainly establish that. Do you mind waiting as it may take me five or ten minutes to check?'

'Not at all, I'm in no hurry.'

After a few minutes she was back.

'I've checked our records and find that M. Vaillant did have both an account and a box with us and the number on the key tallies with our records, but the contents were transferred to a branch in Paris at Place de l'Opéra some years ago. I've asked one of my colleagues to call them to check whether the facilities are still being used.'

It took Peter a moment or two to take in what he had been told.

'So that key was for one of your boxes which he used for personal possessions?'

'Yes the box was first registered in his name in 1970 and the contents were transferred to our Paris branch in 1977. He no longer has an account with this branch.'

The phone in the corner of the room rang and Jane went over to answer it. She then returned to her seat.

'My colleague has just been speaking with our Paris branch and they've confirmed that a safe deposit box exists in M. Vaillant's name and it still holds items that have been lodged there by him. Apparently there is also a small personal account with a modest balance, it has not been used for many years.'

'I really am indebted to you for this information,' said Peter. 'It's taken me a long time to try to find out whether this key signified the existence of a box where my uncle had deposited items for safe keeping – at last I have an answer.'

'I'm pleased we've been able to help. I assume you will ask your lawyers to provide the necessary authorisation to enable our Paris branch to release the contents of the box – they should contact a M. Bernier at our 2 Place de l'Opéra branch.'

'Yes, of course, and once again many thanks for your help, I am most grateful.'

Peter picked up a cab outside the bank and on the way to his flat he called Richard Anstruther.

'Richard, it's Peter. I'm back from France and have a great deal to tell you about my meetings with Delphine. I've also established that the key I found in the packing case was for a safe deposit box here in London but it was closed some years ago and the contents were transferred to a branch of BNP Paribas in Paris. However, it appears likely that the box still contains items Pierre placed there for safe keeping.'

'Well done Peter, I really must give you credit for tenacity in establishing that there still is a safe deposit and also in tracking it down. What are you proposing to do about it now, and do you require anything more from me?'

'Not just at the moment. I had two lengthy meetings with Delphine and have a much clearer picture of the events leading up to Juliette's birth and the relationship between Delphine and

Pierre since then. Apparently Juliette now lives in Paris. After our meeting yesterday, Delphine called to tell her Pierre died last year. I'm planning to give her a call later today to introduce myself and ask if I can meet her in Paris. Whilst I'm there I'll take the opportunity to call on the bank and, with your help, maybe we can get to the bottom of what is stored in that safe deposit. One thing is puzzling me: neither Delphine nor Juliette knew about Pierre's death. I can understand that Delphine might have lost touch with him after her marriage, but I find it surprising that Juliette had no intimation of his declining health. Obviously if their existence was still being kept secret by Pierre, Hubert would have known nothing about them, but Juliette seemed to be unsure whether Pierre was receiving her letters during the last year or two and she gradually stopped hearing from him. It all seems to be very peculiar but until I can talk to Juliette I guess I can't expect to understand how secretive Pierre had been about her existence.'

'It does sound somewhat curious if, as you say, Pierre had grown quite close to her over the years, albeit from afar.'

'I think the only way to find out will be to go to Paris. Have you come across anything more of interest in the files?'

'Yes, I was going to mention a couple of things. There are a lot of papers relating to Pierre's business activities but also some documents dealing with financial arrangements for Delphine and Juliette. However, the real surprise is a document showing that Pierre must have provided funds to enable Delphine to purchase a house in a place called Beuvron.'

'Yes, Delphine mentioned that during our conversation – it's actually where she's still living now. I got the impression the gift probably formalised the end of their relationship because Pierre organised it just before she got married.'

'Pierre was obviously adept at moving large amounts of money around at a time when exchange controls would not have made such arrangements very easy. He really was a man of many parts!'

'I think you're probably right Richard, it seems as though none of us really knew him well, nor what was important to him. But, in the meantime, would you mind organising another letter of authorisation for the BNP Paribas branch at Place de l'Opéra? Hopefully this will be the last time I have to trouble you.'

Back at his flat Peter called the Hotel du Louvre in Paris to check on the availability of rooms. Having satisfied himself that he could book at short notice he called the number he had been given for Juliette.

'Bonjour, c'est Juliette ici.'

'Bonjour Mademoiselle, je suis Peter, le neveu de votre pere Pierre Vaillant. Parlez vous Anglais?'

'Hello Peter. Yes, I am an English teacher. My mother rang me a couple of days ago to tell me you might be calling. She also gave me very sad news about my father's death. Am I right that he died early last year?'

'Yes, apparently his health had been deteriorating for a while, although I only heard the news myself after it had occurred. I would like to come to see you in Paris if it would be convenient, as there are a number of matters the lawyers still need to settle. Might it be possible for me to meet you in a couple of days – I shall be staying at the Hotel du Louvre?'

'That would not be a problem. As we are now in the school holidays I am reasonably free.'

'In that case can we meet at my hotel the day after tomorrow in the morning for coffee?'

'Fine, would 10.30 be convenient?'

'Yes, I look forward to seeing you, I'll book a table so it will be easy to locate me.'

Peter booked a hotel room and reserved a seat on the Eurostar for the following morning. He then called Mark Carter to tell him about his visit to Beuvron and the meeting with Delphine.

'It's good to know she's still well and happy,' said Mark. 'I owe her a great deal for what she did for us in the war. Did your meeting with her help to resolve most of your problems?'

'Yes, although there are still a few loose ends. One thing I meant to ask is whether you kept in touch with Pierre after he left England?'

'Yes we used to chat on the phone occasionally and exchanged birthday and Christmas cards, although I didn't hear from him in the last couple of years, nor could I get through on the phone when I tried calling.'

'I gather he was fairly fragile at the end – maybe he wasn't well enough to write or take calls.'

'You may be right, but I was real sorry not to know what had happened to him until you contacted me. Anyhow, I wish you all the best, keep in touch and do drop in whenever you're in this part of the world.'

Shortly after talking to Mark he received a call from Richard Anstruther.

'We have just come across some papers relating to the sale of Pierre's London business to someone called Branko Dantic.'

'Yes, I've met him.'

'There's nothing particularly unusual – correspondence with the lawyer acting for Pierre and copies of some letters from Branko's lawyer. What is interesting is that it appears that Hubert Young acted as a broker in helping to put the deal together and, according to one of the letters, Pierre suspected him of taking a commission from both sides and possibly giving Branko information that helped him do a better deal. Pierre has scribbled across one of the letters, "Typical of Hubert, always trying to make something more for himself – a nice guy but can he be completely trusted?" It does rather suggest that although Hubert was a friend he was not entirely reliable.'

'That's very interesting,' remarked Peter. 'And it also confirms Mary's view about Hubert.'

'Why, what did she have to say about him?'

'Simply that she felt the same way. I've no idea whether she was just reflecting Pierre's views or maybe she had personal experience of him. Either way, it does rather suggest there's more than meets the eye with Hubert. Meanwhile, I've spoken to Juliette and I'm going to Paris tomorrow. We've arranged to meet the following day.'

'I hope your trip is productive – particularly the visit to the bank.'

'So do I, it's certainly not been easy trying to find out more about the activities of someone with as many secrets as Pierre. I hope to have a clearer picture once I've talked to Juliette, but I'll call you if I hear anything earth-shattering.'

Before leaving the next morning, Peter put Juliette's postcards and Pierre's medals in his bag, together with the silver candlesticks. He arrived at the Eurostar terminal in good time and had a coffee whilst skimming the headlines before boarding. He had used the Eurostar service to get to Paris a number of times previously, but still marvelled at the feat of engineering that took the train underground in England and brought it out in northern France just twenty minutes later.

Once in France, the train started to speed up and cars and lorries on nearby roads were overtaken as if they were stationary. It was now moving so fast that when it encountered the service from Paris en route back to London, Peter noticed that it was passed in just one and a half seconds – a combined speed of 600kph! The journey continued smoothly and, just over three hours after leaving London and following a light lunch, the train pulled in to Gare du Nord. He quickly picked up a taxi driven by a typically taciturn Parisian driver who delivered him outside his hotel, barely acknowledging his presence.

Having checked in, Peter went straight to his room and, after freshening up, decided to stroll across the Tuileries Gardens to the Musée d'Orsay. He always enjoyed the immense space and airiness of the old station building, which offered a perfect environment for what he considered to be one of the finest collections of sculpture and art from the second half of the nineteenth century. He wandered up to the café at roof level and took a tisane out onto the terrace with its great views over the roof tops. 'Such a beautiful city,' he thought, 'it's no surprise that Juliette decided to settle here.'

After manoeuvring his way past groups of tourists and paying his respects to the work of Rodin and Millet, he purchased a few postcards from the shop and then went back to the hotel. Before going for an early supper in a nearby bistro, he had a whisky in the hotel's dimly lit bar but, when he received the bill, he was once again reminded why he now came to Paris much less frequently. However, the French onion soup and the entrecôte steak were both excellent and he got to bed feeling optimistic about the day ahead.

The next morning Peter was up early and wandered along the Seine until he reached Notre Dame on Île de la Cité but then, noticing the time, made his way back to the hotel, passing the Louvre with its stunning glass pyramid. He looked down the Carrousel Gardens to Place de la Concorde and as always was inspired by the character of the Haussmann architecture which created such a stylish backdrop to the gardens and fountains.

He made his way to the lounge a little before 10.30, having told the waiter he was expecting someone to join him, and waited for Juliette with a keen sense of anticipation. A few minutes later a tall, elegant woman in her fifties with auburn hair and dark brown eyes approached his table.

'Peter, I'm Juliette. It's a great pleasure to meet you.'

'It's very kind of you to find the time at such short notice and I'm delighted to see you too. Please make yourself comfortable. Can I get you something to drink?'

'What are you having?'

'I was thinking of having a green tea.'

'I will join you if I may. But first of all please can you tell me more about my father's death?'

'There's not a great deal I can tell you, as I only heard about it last year when I received a letter from his solicitor in Nice telling me he had died and that they were acting as executors of his estate. The funeral had apparently already taken place at a small church in Carros near the villa he used to own and was attended by his mistress, a few friends and one or two ex-business acquaintances. Since then the solicitors have been dealing with the administration of his estate, which was initially delayed until a Will was located. Over the last few months a number of matters have arisen that had to be resolved, one of which led me to track down your mother, who told me about what happened in the war and a little about your life since then. There's a great deal I'd like to know more about, especially after you left Beuvron to live in Paris.'

Whilst he had been talking, Peter had been watching Juliette. She was calm, poised and dressed in that confident way that signalled Parisian chic. A simple black dress with a single row of pearls and matching earrings suggested someone who was sophisticated and self confident. He took an immediate liking to her.

'How much did my mother tell you about me and our relationship with my father?'

'I know you originally believed he was your uncle and I have here the cards you sent him when you went on holiday with your mother.'

Juliette took the cards and read the simple greetings on the reverse.

'I can hardly remember any of these, although I do recall sending cards when we went away. I am so surprised he kept some of them.'

'I also know he visited you occasionally when he was on business trips and that all three of you went on holiday together to Deauville.'

'Yes, that was wonderful. I was beginning to grow up and even had a little flirtation with a boy staying in our hotel. While we were there however, I noticed the relationship between my mother and uncle did not seem to be what I had expected. I sensed they were very close and, when he'd gone back to England, I questioned her about it. Initially she merely said she was very fond of him, but I kept pestering her and, not long after his next visit, she told me he was my father.

'At first, I couldn't fully take in what she had told me, but gradually I became accustomed to the strange situation of having a father in another country and married to someone else. In one respect I think it was easier for my mother once it was out in the open because she could talk more freely about him and her feelings about the situation. However, not long after that I got the impression things were not as they had been. Dad, as I now called him, wrote rather less frequently and seemed to be travelling much further afield on business, often to North Africa and America. Meanwhile, mother became involved with a local man, which I found a little upsetting. He was a very charming person but I thought she was being disloyal.'

'So when you were adopted you already knew Pierre was your father?'

'Yes, mother had finally explained everything two years earlier. He told me later he had always intended it should happen before I was twenty-one.'

'I understand you'd dropped out of university around this time.'

'Yes, I couldn't settle and I had a few emotional problems with young men and also experimented with drugs. I went through a bad patch but Dad turned up in Paris one weekend when I was twenty-four and really helped me to get back on track. We agreed I'd train to become a teacher, which he felt would give me security whether or not I decided later that I wanted to get married. I've always been a very independent person and I liked the idea of a career that was both secure but also doing something worthwhile for the next generation.'

'It's very strange for me to know that I've had a French cousin all this time,' said Peter. 'Especially when I think back to the times when I visited Pierre and had no knowledge of his other life.'

'Dad was very emphatic that nothing was ever to be said about his relationship with my mother. I think he felt guilty about what had happened and especially regretted I hadn't had what he called "a normal childhood".'

'So did you see him fairly frequently after this?'

'Yes, he tried to come to Paris whenever he could and made a point of attending my graduation. For quite some time he'd been telling me that his marriage was not in a good state and I was not surprised when he divorced not long after I got my first teaching post back in Normandy. At the end of the first school year, I spent a few days in London sightseeing and dining in all the restaurants that he claimed were the best for French cuisine. I particularly enjoyed Prunier and Mon Plaisir, but he also insisted that we go to a typically English restaurant which was completely different. I think it was called Rules. It was full of character and I believe he said it was one of London's oldest.'

'I know it very well. Lots of traditional steak pies and puddings – absolutely delicious. Tell me, Juliette, did he talk much about his business activities when you met up with him?'

'Not a great deal, he always seemed to be quite secretive whenever I asked him about business. In the early years after the war, when I was a child, he frequently came to see cheese manufacturers and dairies near Beuvron. Later on, I think he was importing goods from North Africa and I believe he was also involved with an ex-wartime American friend in some business dealings in the United States. He always seemed very restless and ready to try something different. Being an extremely charming person with great charisma, he had no difficulty in making good friends with new business contacts.

'When I was in London for the visit I mentioned, he told me he was thinking of selling his business and moving to the south of France. I tried to persuade him to consider living in Paris, but by now he was in his fifties and I don't think he could face starting up in such a pressurised environment. He told me he had some good contacts in Nice and thought there could be opportunities to sell Normandy dairy products along the Cote D'Azur, so in 1975 he moved down there.'

'I only managed to locate your mother because I came across a number of items, including your postcards and some of her letters, in two packing cases Pierre left at an old friend's house.

Amongst the various files I also found a couple of medals, which I thought you might like to keep, and a pair of silver candlesticks that he was apparently given as a present by one of his suppliers. I keep wondering why he left them there.'

Juliette's eyes filled and she blinked hurriedly a number of times before recovering her composure.

'Thank you for taking the trouble to bring them with you. I'm immensely grateful because the medals have great sentimental value, as they are so closely associated with the time my parents met – I can't tell you how much they mean to me. I don't know why he left things behind – I can only assume he was anxious that anything to do with his past was kept away from prying eyes. Perhaps he hid them because he was worried Mary would find out about us, or even that one of his business colleagues would be inquisitive if they ever came across anything suspicious.'

'You're probably right, because among the papers were details of your adoption and also the arrangements to enable your mother to buy her house. You mentioned his business colleagues – did he ever talk to you about them?'

'Yes, quite often. He mentioned an American whose name was Ted with whom I think he was doing business in America. He also used to be friendly with a local cheese maker near us in Beuvron – it was he who gave Dad the candlesticks. There was also a Croatian whose name I can't remember? Dad described him as being not quite straight but I think he secretly admired his energy and initiative.'

'Was his name Goran?'

'Yes, that's right. Do you know him?'

'No, but I found out that Pierre sold his business to Goran's son when he left England.'

'That's right and another business acquaintance of Dad's was involved, a chap called Hubert Young. I don't think Dad trusted him completely and he wasn't entirely happy about Hubert's involvement with the sale. He once mentioned to me that Hubert may have given Goran's son information that should have been kept confidential.'

'That's interesting, there was a comment in one of your father's files about Hubert which was not particularly complimentary. I'm rather surprised that when Hubert sold his business in England, Pierre invited him to work at the vineyard.'

'But that's not what happened. Hubert sold up and then asked Dad if he could join him in Nice to relax and decide what he wanted to do with the rest of his life. Apparently Hubert just turned up one morning, having gone down on the night sleeper, and he became a house guest for the next couple of weeks. He asked Dad for a job and claimed he could make a big contribution to the expansion of the business.'

'That's most intriguing, because I went to see Hubert at the villa about ten days ago and he gave me the impression that Pierre had taken him on in order to keep an eye on things. However, maybe we could talk a little more about that later because I'd really like to know more about the time when Pierre first moved back to France.'

'Well you know how energetic he was, Peter. He rented a flat on the Quai des Etats-Unis and was soon supplying many of the major supermarkets in and around Nice with dairy products. He always did a great deal of entertaining, particularly the buyers of the big chains. After he'd been in Nice for a few years he told me he'd noticed there were hardly any cheap local wines available in the supermarkets, so he contacted a number of local growers and asked if they would like him to represent them. Two of them appointed him to become their agent and apparently he had considerable success on their behalf.

'Not long after, one of them, who was thinking of retiring and whose vineyard was near Carros, asked if he would be interested in buying it. Dad jumped at the chance and that's when the Vaillant label came into existence. Once Dad took over it was even more successful and shortly after that he bought the villa. He often used to ring me in those days and always talked with pride about the quality of his rosé, which seemed to be very popular. On occasions I went to stay in Nice during the summer but, in order to maintain Dad's subterfuge, I was always introduced as the daughter of one of his friends in northern France.'

'But why do you think he was still hiding the fact you were his daughter?'

'I suspect it had become an ingrained habit. He had become so accustomed to keeping both mother's and my existence secret that he couldn't bring himself to explain to his friends that he'd been living a lie for such a long time. He had a certain standing in the community in Nice and I think he felt that if he was seen to have behaved badly, it could affect his business. Such things are now very common in France, but Dad came from a generation that had very inflexible ideas about behaviour and morality. I think he was also concerned about something else from his past to which he didn't want to draw attention, so he avoided any situation that could invite questions.'

Peter wondered whether this might be an appropriate point to mention the safe deposit box and its possible contents, but decided to talk about it later.

'Do you know how he met Helene Martin?'

'Yes, I think Hubert introduced them. Helene was wine buyer for a group of local supermarkets and became an important customer. Hubert had been building up the relationship with her and she was beginning to place large orders for their chain. Dad told me later that Hubert had suggested taking her to dinner to thank her for the business and to strengthen the relationship. Helene was a little younger than Dad, a glamorous dyed blonde divorcee who wore a lot of jewellery and even more perfume. I think Dad took the role of grateful supplier a little too seriously because not long after that she apparently became more than just a customer!'

'When was this?'

'I can't remember exactly – maybe ten or twelve years ago.'

'I gather they used to go gambling in Monte Carlo quite frequently.'

'Yes, I must confess that concerned me. I know from what Dad told me he'd occasionally played blackjack and roulette at clubs in London, and Helene had been used to getting her escorts to take her to dinner in Monte Carlo and then indulging her at the tables. At first they went infrequently but I got the impression that once their relationship became more permanent, she asked him to take her there at least a couple of times a month. I don't think he lost very much but it didn't seem to me to be something she should be encouraging.'

'That's interesting, because when I called to see Hubert he gave me the impression Pierre was a heavy gambler and a big loser, which was one of the main reasons he had to sell the business and the villa.'

'Well, Dad never mentioned that to me but I guess over time his losses might have mounted up. I never liked Helene much and I don't think she had Dad's best interests at heart. Quite apart from the gambling, she was what I think you'd call "high maintenance". He paid for her flat and gave her an allowance, but even then she often asked him to buy her clothes and jewellery – it's probably not a surprise that he started to have some financial problems.'

'Did he ever discuss them with you?'

'No, as far as I was aware everything was fine. However, over the last few years we didn't have as much contact as in the past. It's a bit difficult to maintain a relationship that's so unorthodox, and Dad came to Paris less frequently. He had a bit of a health scare in 1999 and I think that slowed him down quite a lot. It also became more difficult for me to spend time with him in Nice once Helene became such a permanent part of his life, as she was quite nosy and was apparently always asking questions about me, which obviously made him feel uncomfortable.'

'When I met your mother I got the impression from her that you lost touch with him during the last couple of years and that he wasn't replying to your letters, which seems a bit strange. I wonder if he was suffering from Alzheimer's or something similar.'

'I just don't know. But I was aware that, for some reason or other, the business was doing so badly that he had to sell it as well as the villa. He did some sort of deal with Hubert but he didn't tell me any of the details. In the last letter I received from him he told me he was going to be living in the lodge at the beginning of the drive, which meant he could still enjoy the garden, but not long after that I stopped getting replies to my letters and couldn't reach him on the phone.'

'Didn't you think that was strange?'

'Yes, I did, although he'd always been a bit haphazard with communication. I often didn't hear from him for months, then he'd call and we would talk for an hour or more. I suppose I was used to not hearing from him very often once he got involved with Helene and I was pretty busy with friends and school trips that took me abroad quite a lot. Looking back, I feel quite bad about not taking more trouble to find out what was happening, but we'd always had a very detached relationship so I suppose it's not entirely surprising. I do find it very strange, though, that I didn't get replies to my letters and the phone connection seemed to be faulty for such a long time.'

'Do you think it's possible that Helene Martin or Hubert knew more about Pierre's past than they've revealed?'

'I really don't know, but once Dad became ill I suppose it's possible Hubert started prying among his papers at the villa.'

'Do you think he might have come across some of your letters?'

'I think it's unlikely, as Dad said he always shredded them once he'd read them.'

'But what about letters you wrote to him when he was ill or in the last few months before he died?'

'I hadn't considered that. I probably wrote two or three times without getting a reply which, as I said earlier, I thought a little strange, but given Dad's involvement with Helene it didn't worry me unduly. Now, with the benefit of hindsight, it seems very odd indeed.'

'When you couldn't get through on the phone, did you try calling Hubert to check on the situation?'

'Yes, he just said there was a problem with the line at the lodge and that getting an engineer to check a line outside Nice always took forever. He said Dad was fine although somewhat fragile and getting forgetful, but he promised to pass on my good wishes.'

Peter caught the eye of a waiter. 'Would you like another green tea?'

'I rather think I'd like something a little stronger – is it too early for a glass of white wine?'

'Not at all, how about a Chablis?'

'That would be perfect. Remind me Peter, how did you hear about Dad's death?'

'I had a letter from his solicitor in London who'd been contacted by Maître Simon. I think it was about ten days after he died and the funeral had apparently already taken place.'

'Weren't you surprised not to have heard sooner?'

'I was rather, although I hadn't had much contact with him recently.'

'You know, the more we talk about this, Peter, the more I begin to wonder if there could be anything suspicious about the circumstances surrounding the sale of the vineyard and the villa.'

'Well, according to Hubert, it came after a very bad year for the vineyard and some significant losses at the casino.'

'I know, but nonetheless, do you think it's possible that Helene was collaborating with Hubert in some way to force a sale?'

'How do you mean?'

'Well, suppose they knew about me. If so they would be aware that under French law legal priority is given to what are known as "héritiers réservataires" or "protected heirs", and that I would be the principal beneficiary of Dad's estate. They stood to gain by acquiring the business at a reduced price before he died and I could inherit. Do you know anything else about the sudden need to sell?'

'Only that they'd had a bad year and, as I mentioned, Pierre may have had some big gambling losses. Wait a minute, Hubert said there was also a big order from a supermarket group which was cancelled at the last minute as they were not able to fulfil it. According to Hubert, the wine harvest was so poor they would only have been able to satisfy two thirds of the order. However, once that order was cancelled they were left with a large amount of stock which had to be sold off cheaply.'

'Is it possible that Hubert might have accepted the order in the knowledge that it was well in excess of their capacity and couldn't be fulfilled, thereby precipitating a crisis which could lead to a forced sale?'

'It's certainly possible and would have exacerbated an already difficult situation.'

'And if Helene was encouraging Dad to gamble and he was losing heavily that would have put him under even more financial pressure.'

'I can certainly imagine it could be easy to lose quite a lot of money very quickly if he was unlucky. I went to the casino in Monte Carlo a couple of weeks ago to try to get a feeling for the environment. If she was encouraging him to go regularly he could have made some very sizeable losses.'

'Just going back to that supermarket order, Peter, wouldn't you have thought that when they realised it couldn't be fulfilled, they might have scaled back all their other orders so they wouldn't lose it?'

'I agree, but maybe they didn't want to upset all their other customers. Mind you, if what you are implying is true, it suited Hubert to have it cancelled. I wonder if the supermarket was the one with which Mme Martin was originally involved.'

'Presumably that could be checked, but I don't know that it proves anything.'

'Only that she might have used her past connections to encourage them to place a much larger order, knowing it would be a problem and would create a financial crisis which could push Pierre into a situation where he felt he had no alternative but to sell.'

'But wouldn't Pierre have realised that the order was beyond their capacity?'

'Yes, but don't forget he had been ill and was presumably relying more and more on Hubert.'

'I must say, I find this all very disconcerting, particularly if Dad was forced into selling the business and the villa by subterfuge.'

'Why don't we forget this for the moment and I'll make some enquiries about the supermarket that cancelled the order when I get back home. The good news is that the solicitors in London have documentary evidence that you are Pierre's daughter and, as you mentioned earlier, that establishes your claim to his estate. It may not be quite so valuable as it was before the sale of the business but I suspect it's still quite sizeable.'

'That's not the point Peter, I'm concerned that Hubert and possibly Helene may have behaved in an underhand way, which is very distressing in view of everything Dad did for them.'

'I'll make some discreet enquiries about the cancelled order, Juliette, but in the meantime can I mention something which emerged in one of your mother's letters to Pierre? I asked her about this when we met and, for reasons I don't fully understand, she was reluctant to discuss it with me. Do you know anything about a safe deposit box at BNP Paribas, the contents of which were transferred from London to Paris?'

'Yes, I do, but how did you find out about it?'

'I discovered a key marked "BNP" in one of the packing cases Pierre had stored in Wiltshire and, having made enquiries in London, I was told that the contents are at the Place de l'Opéra branch. A letter of authorisation from the London solicitors will enable me to access the contents, but before going there I wondered if you knew what they contained.'

Juliette took in a deep breath and did not speak for a few moments.

CHAPTER NINE

'PETER, SINCE YOU'VE asked me and you're planning to visit the bank I'll tell you what I know. You may be aware that in the war, Dad was an agent working with the Resistance in Normandy, where he was responsible for planning and executing attacks on strategic targets such as communications installations, bridges, railways and munitions trains. It was after he'd been dropped into their area that he met my mother, who was an active Resistance fighter, and they undertook a number of operations both before and after the Normandy Landings.

'Apparently, one night shortly after D-Day, Dad and an explosives expert used roadside bombs to blow up a car, which they had been told was carrying three senior SS tank commanders to a briefing meeting at their headquarters in Paris. The explosion wrecked the car, killing the occupants, and when Dad searched the debris to see if he could find military information which might be useful to London, he found two badly battered metal briefcases. Minutes later, a German personnel carrier appeared and Dad and his companion fled in different directions. Much later, when he was back in his room in my grandparents' house he prised open the cases. One contained plans for a counter-attack against advancing allied forces on Sword Beach, the other some maps, a number of rather unsavoury photographs, two boxes of cigars, a hip flask containing brandy and two soft leather pouches, a small one containing diamonds, the other considerably larger which was full of French Napoleon gold coins.

'He told me that at first he was elated by his discovery, but later felt remorse at the thought that the valuables which had fallen into his hands had been stolen and that it would be impossible to find their owners. He realised he had to find somewhere to hide them and decided to bury the two pouches in a nearby wood. Having done this, he went back to the house, where he encountered my mother, who had just returned from an operation. Apparently he told her that, during an attack on a military vehicle, he had found a package containing some valuables and that he'd buried them nearby for safe keeping. He said he intended to leave them buried until German forces had left the area. As you probably know, not long after that mother was captured and imprisoned.'

'So do you think they might be in the safe deposit box at the bank?'

'I really don't know. I asked him once what he'd done with them when he got back to England. He was a bit cagy but I got the impression he'd cashed some of the coins to finance his business in the early days in London. He may have used more of them to provide funds to buy the house for mother, but I don't know whether anything is left or what else may be lodged with the bank.'

'What an extraordinary story. Now it's clear what your mother was referring to in a letter she sent him after her release when she asked about a package he had hidden. She was very reluctant to discuss this with me when I mentioned it to her.'

'I suspect that was because Dad felt uncomfortable about what he'd found and also the circumstances in which he acquired them. Of course, he was very young and it was a time of war, but he was understandably reluctant to talk much about it. They were also still involved in operations, so probably had little time to think of anything else.'

'Juliette, I'm intending to go to the bank this afternoon. I wonder if you'd like to come with me, since whatever we find there is part of Pierre's estate and you'll now be the principal beneficiary.'

'What time are you planning to be there, as I'm meeting a friend for lunch?'

'I thought I'd go at around three o'clock. Would that be convenient for you? It's the Place de l'Opéra branch.'

'That would give me plenty of time. Shall I meet you there?'

'Yes, and in the meantime I'll call the solicitor in London and see what more we can find out about the supermarket that cancelled the large order which precipitated the sale of the business.'

'Au revoir, then, Peter. I'll see you at the bank this afternoon.'

Peter went up to his room and sat thinking about their conversation and in particular the circumstances surrounding the sale of Pierre's business and the villa. He concluded that he needed to get a better idea of the financial position of the company just before the enforced sale, as well as more information about the cancelled supermarket order. He dialled Richard Anstruther and was put through by his secretary.

'Richard, it's Peter. I've spent the last couple of hours with Juliette and, as you can probably imagine, it's been absolutely fascinating. I won't go into it all just now, but it does seem there was something not entirely straightforward about the sale of Pierre's business to Hubert Young. Juliette thinks that he and possibly Helene Martin may have found out about her and realised she would be the principal beneficiary from Pierre's estate. So it's just possible they might have planned to force the sale of the business by precipitating a crisis over the large supermarket order that was cancelled and led to financial problems. It may be that the situation was made worse by Pierre's gambling, which seems to have been encouraged by Helene Martin. In view of this, I wonder if you might be able to get someone in Maître Simon's office in Nice to get us more information about the state of the company's finances immediately before the sale, and also the precise circumstances of the cancelled order, which was clearly very sizeable. It would be particularly useful to find out whether Helene Martin had any connection with that company in the past, as apparently she was the buyer for a supermarket group before she met Pierre.'

'You certainly seem to have covered a lot of ground, Peter – I'll see what I can do. Meanwhile, is there any more information about the mysterious safe deposit box?'

'I'm going to the bank this afternoon, so I should finally have some answers later on. Do they have the necessary authorisation to give me access?'

'Yes, although they'll almost certainly require some form of indemnity from us before you can remove anything.'

'That's fine. Richard, there is one other small thing. Do you think there's any way of establishing the scale of Pierre's losses at the casino?'

'Not that I can think of immediately. He presumably purchased chips with cash, and there is no way a casino can identify individual losses on a roulette table so long after the event. A camera records individual bets on each spin of the wheel in case there's a subsequent dispute, but they wouldn't keep records from so long ago. However, if he was a regular visitor, and someone they considered to be a high roller, they might have cashed cheques for him. I'll look into it. How much longer do you plan to stay?'

'Well, as I mentioned, I'm going to the bank this afternoon and will probably return to London tomorrow, unless there's any need for me to stay.'

'Very good, I'll see what we can find out about the financial state of the company before its sale and, if possible, more about the supermarket contract. In the meantime I'm looking forward to hearing what you finally unearth in that safe deposit box.'

Peter had a quick lunch at a nearby bistro. An excellent steak with pommes frites and a side salad accompanied by a glass of Merlot and followed by a coffee. As always, he was impressed by the flavour of the coffee which seemed to be so much better than in London. He then took a leisurely stroll up Avenue de l'Opéra and, arriving at the Opera building, decided to check on the evening's performance and also whether he might be able to obtain a ticket. The posters showed that *La Bohème* was to be performed, although unfortunately no tickets were available. At the desk, it was suggested he might consider coming back in the evening in the event of returns. He decided he wouldn't bother and wandered down the steps and across to the bank to wait for Juliette. Just beside the bank, a middle-aged woman sat on the pavement with a dog dressed up in a costume that would not have looked out of place in the opera house. She had a cassette from which popular arias were playing for the amusement of passers-by, many of whom put a coin in a cup placed immediately in front of the dog. The performance was clearly appreciated as the cup quickly filled in the short time Peter waited. A few minutes later Juliette joined him outside the bank.

'If I'd been here another ten minutes I might have heard something from *La Bohème*,' said Peter, pointing to the woman with the dog.

'Oh she's here quite often, I suspect she earns more than the members of the chorus!'

They walked into the bank and over to the reception desk, where Peter explained the reason for the visit and showed their letter of authorisation. As was now becoming customary, they were taken to a meeting room and asked to wait.

A few minutes later a bank clerk came into the room and asked for identification. Peter and Juliette both produced their passports which were checked and handed back to them. They waited again and after a short while were joined by a middle-aged man who introduced himself in English as Paul Bernier, one of the bank's assistant managers.

'Good afternoon Mademoiselle Leger and Monsieur Barton. I have received a communication from your solicitors in London and can confirm that Monsieur Vaillant closed the small account he had at this branch a while ago and transferred the funds to a bank in Nice. However, we are holding certain items on his behalf in one of our deposit boxes. If you would like to follow me I will take you to a private room adjacent to our secure area where you can inspect the contents.'

They followed him down to the basement and were shown into a small room which had a table and two chairs alongside what looked like a closed serving hatch above a shelf.

'Would you mind waiting here for a couple of moments? I am about to enter a secure area to which customers are not permitted entry. As you are not the owners of the box, I should explain that the procedure for examining items stored with the bank is as follows. The box will be passed through to you for inspection, together with a form summarising its contents, which you should sign. When you hand the box back, we will give you a receipt confirming it is once again in the bank's custody. You will understand that in order to release the contents of the box we will, of course, require additional documents from your solicitor, indemnifying the bank against any subsequent claims.'

M. Bernier left the room and Peter observed, 'I suppose all this bureaucracy is necessary. I guess it ensures they are never accused of releasing valuable items into the wrong hands.'

A few moments later, the hatch door slid across and M. Bernier held out the form for signature.

'Shall we both sign?' said Peter.

'That is not necessary, one signature will suffice.'

Peter handed back the paper and what appeared to be a rectangular metal container with a drawer was placed on the counter.

'When you are finished, please ring the bell beside the table. You will not be disturbed.'

The door to the hatch was closed.

Peter put the container on the desk and pulled out the drawer. In it was a small leather valise with the initials 'PLV'.

He passed it to Juliette. 'You should open it.'

She started to remove the contents. First came an envelope containing photographs, many of which were of her at various ages and in different places, others of Delphine and two or three showing Pierre, Juliette and Delphine together, one of which appeared to be at a holiday resort.

'That's our holiday together in Deauville which I told you about. Dad must have been anxious to keep these away from prying eyes.'

Next, a much larger envelope with a number of letters which Juliette put to one side. Another envelope contained old newspaper cuttings which related to the award of the Médaille de la Résistance to a number of Free French operatives including Pierre.

'Dad never mentioned that his award had been covered by the media.'

'Maybe he wanted to put that period of his life behind him.'

Juliette now took out a leather pouch, pulled tight and knotted at the top. She undid the knot and poured the contents – an assortment of uncut diamonds – onto the table. They both looked at the stones in amazement and then each became aware of the expression of surprise on the other's face. For a few moments they were both speechless.

'It's incredible, these must be what Dad discovered during the attack on that car all those years ago.'

'I can hardly believe it,' said Peter. 'I imagine they must be, although we have no way of knowing. I don't know much about diamonds, but some of these stones are quite large and must be valuable.'

'What should we do about them, Peter?'

'I don't think there is anything we can do, it was all so long ago. If they'd been cut and mounted in rings or pieces of jewellery it might be possible to locate the original owners, but in this form they are untraceable. It really is quite extraordinary that these have been locked away for so long and have finally come to light as a result of finding that key back in the packing case in England.'

Juliette had pulled one other item from the case. It was an envelope with her name on it.

'Is that everything?' said Peter.

'Yes, I'll just go through the contents of the other envelope before I open this.'

She spent a few minutes reading the various letters and other items whilst Peter looked through the photographs again.

'There are two or three letters from mother following Dad's visits: one thanking him for a car he gave her, another talking about my adoption. She also writes to him about the money he gave her to buy the house. He seems to have kept a number of my letters, especially one that I wrote after he adopted me. That photograph you're holding is of the three of us and was taken the night we had dinner together to celebrate at Dad's favourite restaurant in Caen. He's even kept a copy of my last school report, which mother must have sent him. I'd forgotten the final comment, "Juliette has great potential but is a bit of a dreamer. She has good communication skills but needs to be more focused if she is to be successful." – in retrospect it was probably correct!'

Juliette now opened the letter which was addressed to her and started to read. After a few moments tears filled her eyes and she briefly stopped reading.

'What is it?' said Peter.

'Let me finish and then I'll explain.'

She returned to the letter and reread it before putting it down.

'Are you able to share it with me?' said Peter.

'A lot of it is quite personal. He talks about his regrets that we had such an unorthodox relationship and that he never faced the consequences of his actions by not acknowledging Mother and me publicly. He recalls many of the happy moments we had together and expresses pride in what I've achieved after a somewhat difficult period in my twenties. There's a brief mention about his time in France in the war and he explains again how the diamonds came to be in his possession. Whilst accepting that the way in which they were acquired was wrong, he points out that in wartime many things occurred which are difficult to defend.'

She broke off for a moment and apologised.

'I'm sorry, he goes on to talk rather emotionally about what he achieved in building up his business in the south of France and reiterates that he wishes he had not been so obsessed with concealing my identity, which meant my visits to Nice were never relaxed and often quite uncomfortable. There are some comments about Helene Martin which are not particularly flattering, although he recognises that as an elderly man he has to accept that he's now rather dependent on her. Interestingly, he implies that the sale of the company was unavoidable due to financial problems. He then goes on to say he hopes the diamonds may compensate me for what I lost in not having a normal family life. The letter finishes with him expressing fears he is beginning to lose his memory, that there are problems with the phone and that he has sent this letter to his bank as he doesn't want me to read it until he is dead.'

'That's very sad, but his loss of memory may account for the absence of communication in the final months,' said Peter.'

'I'm sure you're right. But it is very sad, and I feel I should have made more of an effort to contact him, although I assumed he was in good hands with Helene and Hubert.'

'You mustn't reproach yourself in view of the unusual circumstances. However, there's something that mystifies me about what we've found here today. How could Pierre be sure we'd find this box and its contents, especially as you didn't know of its existence?'

'Is it possible that, since Dad was not prepared to reveal my existence, he may have talked to Helene about the packing cases knowing she would want to investigate further? Didn't you say that she'd hired a private detective to try to find out more about them?'

'That seems a bit haphazard to me. However, perhaps M. Bernier can throw some more light on the matter. Meanwhile, we'd better list everything so the solicitors can make a formal request for the items to be released into their custody.'

'But what about the personal letters, Peter?'

'Well, having found the papers relating to your adoption, both firms of solicitors know all about you so there are no great revelations among the letters. I hardly think M. Bernier would notice if one of them was missing, so why don't you slip the one you've just been reading into your bag?'

Peter rang the bell, the door to the hatch slid across and Peter passed the tray and valise back. After a minute or two M. Bonnard appeared.

'I have the countersigned form but we notice that a letter has been removed.'

'I'm to blame,' said Peter. 'It was a letter addressed to Mlle Leger and we therefore took it to be her property.'

'In the circumstances I quite understand, but you realise I had to raise the matter.'

'Of course,' said Peter. 'I would like to query something with you if I may. In view of the fact that M. Vaillant no longer has an account with the bank, I wonder how his executors would have known of the existence of this safe deposit had I not found out about it. Is there some mechanism in place that notifies the next of kin of someone who has opened a deposit box in secrecy and subsequently dies without anyone knowing anything about it?'

'Such situations are rare, but occasionally someone dies without any known next of kin. Normally there is a bank account and from that it is possible to trace executors but if, as in M. Vaillant's case, the account has been closed for some time, we review our records of visits to inspect boxes in our system and would make discreet enquiries to establish the whereabouts of an owner. We like to think that the contents of a box owned by someone who has died will ultimately always be reunited with whoever may be entitled to them. Now, is there anything else I can do to assist and, most importantly, have you noted the contents so that you can make the necessary application to enable us to release them to the executors in due course?'

'Yes, and thank you again, you've been most helpful,' said Peter. 'We've seen everything we require just at the moment.'

Leaving the bank Juliette proposed a short walk to have tea at Fauchon at Place de la Madeleine.

'It's a little like your Fortnum & Mason – a temple to fine food. I think you'll enjoy it.'

Once they were in the restaurant and settled at a quiet table. Juliette studied the menu.

'I was hoping we might be fortunate. At about this time of the year they have their eclair week, when there are more than thirty different types of eclair to choose from. They come in spectacular designs, one of which is a chocolate coated facsimile of the *Mona Lisa*! But sadly today we are not in luck. If you like pastries, I recommend a Paris-Brest, shaped like a bicycle wheel and filled with cream, almond praline, hazelnut paste and topped with almonds – absolutely delicious!'

'I love cakes and am especially fortunate that my former PA very generously bakes me the most sensational cake every Christmas – I've sometimes been able to make it last until the New Year! Your recommendation sounds wonderful, but what will you have?'

'I think a pot of English tea would be a treat and, in view of where we are, I'll have some Madeleine biscuits.'

Having ordered, Juliette took out the letter from her father and glanced through it again.

'Do you think I am being paranoid, Peter, or do you share my view that there seems to be something very strange about the circumstances surrounding the sale to Hubert of Dad's company and also the villa?'

'I must confess, I think it needs to be looked at more closely and I've asked Richard Anstruther, the solicitor in London, to make enquiries into the background to the sale. I'm pretty sure that, in the light of what we now know, it'll be reasonably easy to find out exactly what happened. Once I'm back in London and have had the chance to talk to him I think I may have to return to Nice. But in the meantime, Juliette, have you given any thought to the diamonds in the safe deposit box?'

'They've been worrying me ever since we found them. I realise they can't be returned to their original owners but I feel very uneasy about possessing something that's not mine, especially if they're valuable. Fortunately I don't have to worry about them just at the moment, although I guess they'll become part of Dad's estate and, as a result, the inheritance tax bill will be considerably higher. So I presume they'll have to be sold to cover that.'

'I think you're probably right, Juliette, but I suspect it's a matter for the lawyers. By the way, this pastry is sensational.'

'I'm glad you're enjoying it, they're very popular with Parisians.'

A waitress approached to enquire whether they required anything else and Peter asked for the bill.

'I think I should get back to my hotel to talk to Richard Anstruther about making a formal application for the removal of the contents of the box. I also want to talk to him about Pierre's comments concerning the financial problems that arose prior to the sale. But perhaps most important, I seem to have finally finished what I started out to do and now have the feeling I'm interfering in what is really your business.'

'But Peter, without your efforts it could've been ages before the safe deposit was discovered and any rights I now have as Dad's heir were recognised. I owe you a huge debt of gratitude.'

'Juliette, I'm only too pleased to have been able to help.'

They walked out into the late afternoon sunshine.

'Peter, do you mind if I ask whether you know what is in Dad's Will?'

'Broadly yes. The estate is smaller than might've been expected because of the financial problems and obviously everything changes now you've become his heir. He made provision for Helene Martin to receive a bequest and an income for life from a portfolio that would ultimately revert to a charity, he left his not inconsiderable cellar to Hubert, there were a number of other small bequests to friends including his ex-wife Mary and Suzanne, Mme Martin's daughter, and the balance was left to me.'

'So what happens now?'

'Well, as I said, I need to get back to London so I can bring Richard Anstruther up to date with our conversations and also what we found in the safe deposit. I also want to see what he's been able to find out about the sale of the business to Hubert. There's just one thing you and I need to agree upon – what is to be said about the diamonds. My feeling is that as this all took place nearly sixty years ago, the past is the past. I don't think it's for you or me to judge Pierre's actions in a time of war, as there was no way the original owners could be traced. For that reason I feel we should merely refer to them as something that Pierre must have acquired as an investment and kept at the bank for safety. What do you think?'

'Peter, I think you're right that the circumstances relating to them coming into Dad's possession should remain our secret. However, I'd like to think a little more about what should happen to the proceeds when they are sold.'

'That's fine Juliette, I'll simply tell Richard we found some uncut diamonds that Pierre must have purchased as an investment.'

They were now back at Peter's hotel.

'I'm going to book the early train tomorrow morning, so should be back in London before lunch and will try to see Richard in the afternoon. Would you like me to give you a call after I've seen him?'

'That would be very kind, Peter. It's been such a pleasure meeting my English cousin and I hope we're going to become very good friends in future. I can't tell you how much I appreciate what you've done to help me, but hopefully when everything is resolved we can meet again in more relaxed circumstances either here or in London, so I can reciprocate your kindness.'

'It's been a pleasure, Juliette. Au revoir, I'll ring you tomorrow evening.'

CHAPTER TEN

PETER FELT IN need of a drink and sat in the hotel bar with a glass of whisky for company. He decided that, whatever Richard Anstruther managed to find out about Hubert's activities, he would go back to Nice to make some enquiries himself. He felt certain his advice to Juliette about the diamonds was correct, despite the manner in which they had been acquired, but couldn't stop wondering what effect her claim to the estate would have on his own legacy. Putting these thoughts out of his head, he returned to his room and called Eurostar to book a seat on the morning train to London. Next he made a call to Richard's secretary.

'Is there any chance of half an hour with Richard later tomorrow afternoon?'

'He could see you at four o'clock or, if that's not possible, eleven o'clock the following morning.'

'Tomorrow at four o'clock would be fine, I'll see him then.'

He decided to send Delphine a card to tell her about his meeting with Juliette and on an impulse he sent one to Suzanne with the simple message 'Greeting from Paris'.

Still feeling the after-effects of his pastry, he walked over to the Louvre and spent a while meandering through some of its galleries. As he hadn't been able to sample the eclair with the reproduction of its image, he decided the original would be even more rewarding, so he made his way to the gallery where a crowd encircled the *Mona Lisa*. After contemplating her somewhat ambiguous smile, which invariably left him bemused, he realised the museum was about to close, so he returned to the hotel and wrote another couple of cards, one to Mary, which conveyed little more than greetings, the other to Mark, thanking him again for his past help. As he was now feeling tired and didn't want to bother to go out to dinner, he called room service and ordered an omelette with a salad and some cheese to follow. Since he had to make an early start he decided against drinking wine or coffee and confined himself to a bottle of Evian. Shortly afterwards, having watched the news, he went to bed.

The next morning a rather more sociable taxi driver dropped him at the station and, by half past ten, he was already travelling across the Kent countryside, having enjoyed an excellent English breakfast. The train made good time and he was back in his flat just after midday. He unpacked, putting the list of the contents of the safe deposit box on his desk, and listened to the messages on his answerphone. None of them appeared to be particularly important, apart from a client who wanted to arrange a lunch later in the month to discuss a business project and a rather rambling call from Hubert enquiring whether he was making any progress and if he had any news. Peter wondered what the motive was for the call but had no intention of returning it before he had his meeting with Richard Anstruther.

After a late lunch at a nearby pub, and feeling in need of exercise, he strolled up Sloane Street and crossed into the park before cutting across to Curzon Street. As it was only 3.30 he stopped for a cup of coffee in Berkeley Square and arrived in Old Burlington Street just before four o'clock.

'How was the trip to Paris?' said Richard as he walked into the meeting room.

'Very interesting. I liked Juliette enormously. She's bright and sensible and seems to be thoroughly well balanced despite her rather curious upbringing. It's rather odd to find one has a cousin and then to meet her for the first time in such circumstances.'

'What did you find in the safe deposit box?'

'A number of photos and letters to Pierre from Delphine. There was also a letter addressed to Juliette – mostly personal stuff, but Pierre specifically commented on the circumstances of the sale of the company and implied that it had not been entirely straightforward. There were also some uncut diamonds which I guess he regarded as an investment.'

'Really, do you know what they might be worth?'

'I'm afraid not. I haven't any idea of the value of uncut stones, but I have a list of them together with the other items, so that you or Maître Simon can make a formal application for them to be released.'

'I think that's best left to Maître Simon but I'll get on to it right away. I imagine she'll want to sell them and, in any event, there'll be a pretty sizeable amount of tax to pay on the proceeds.'

'I would guess so, Richard, although she hasn't said anything to me about them.'

'How is she taking the news that he's dead and that she'll be the main beneficiary of the estate?'

'It's difficult to tell. It must be very strange, especially as she hadn't heard from him for a couple of years. I think she found the circumstances surrounding the end of his life very suspicious, especially as she didn't get replies to letters and couldn't talk to him on the phone, but I imagine she'd become accustomed to a very clandestine relationship. By the way, have you been able to find out anything more about the sale of the business?'

'Not as much as I'd hoped, but there could be some more information tomorrow. I've been able to establish that the performance of the company had not been so good in the two years prior to it being sold and bank borrowing had increased, secured against a personal guarantee given by Pierre. Apparently they had a very poor crop, borrowings increased further and then the problem arose with the large order that was cancelled, leaving them with stock that had to be cleared very cheaply.'

'Were you able to find out whether there's any connection between Helene Martin and the supermarket that cancelled the order?'

'I'm still waiting for information about that and also Pierre's casino losses – hopefully I'll have more news in the morning.'

'In that case I'll give you a call tomorrow and, subject to what you find out, I'll probably go back to Nice to see if I can finally tie up the loose ends.'

'That's fine, Peter. I'll await your call.'

Back at his flat, Peter rang Juliette and told her about the meeting with Richard. He mentioned he was thinking of going back to Nice and asked whether she had made any decisions about the diamonds.

'Not yet, I think I'll wait until they're with the solicitors and have been valued, but I assume they'll have to be sold to cover tax liabilities on the estate. However, I have been thinking about all the time you've spent tracking down Mother and me and also locating the safe deposit. I really can't understand why you went to so much trouble.'

'Maybe you could say it was initially self-interest as I was the main beneficiary from Pierre's Will, but I was also trying to clear up what appeared to be a bit of a mystery. As I got more involved I wanted to find out about Pierre's hidden life, which I must confess I've found very intriguing. I guess all that now remains to be checked out is the real story behind the sale of his business.'

'But everything has changed – it makes me feel rather guilty about my situation.'

'Don't be silly, Juliette, you deserve your inheritance much more than I'd have done.'

'I need time to think about this, Peter. Can we talk when everything is finalised?'

'Of course, you can call me any time, either here or on my mobile.'

The next morning, Peter was sitting in his study reading some business papers when the phone rang. It was Richard.

'I have some very interesting information, is it a good time to talk?'

'I'm all ears.'

'Right, first of all Helene Martin used to be the buyer for the supermarket group that cancelled the order and is very friendly with the person who replaced her. My sources tell me the two of them frequently lunched together and have even been away on shopping trips to Paris.'

'How extraordinary. It sounds rather too cosy to me.'

'But there's more, Peter. The large order which was subsequently cancelled was placed just after the previous year's poor harvest. The order was much larger than any previously from that supermarket and, together with others, was well in excess of the vineyard's capacity.'

'So even if it hadn't been cancelled it would've been too large for them to handle?'

'Exactly, but in cancelling it they compounded the problem.'

'Is there any way we can find out more about how and why they placed such a large order?'

'I've asked that question and I'm hoping to have more information later today.'

'But this really does suggest there might've been a conspiracy to create a financial crisis and force the sale of the company.'

'It certainly looks like it, but there's something else. Hubert had borrowed money from the company prior to all this, hence the need for additional bank borrowing.'

'But why would Pierre have agreed to the loans?'

'I've no idea, unless he was too unwell to argue.'

'Or else because he was being pressurised.'

'What do you mean, Peter?'

'Well, suppose Hubert had found out about Juliette and was threatening to disclose what he knew?'

'I see what you mean.'

'Having kept the story secret all his life and not now wanting to embarrass Juliette, Pierre might have agreed to the loans as a form of pay-off to ensure that Hubert kept quiet.'

'I suppose that's possible, but I'm not sure how we can prove it.'

'Well, if you can get more information about the dealings between Helene Martin and the supermarket buyer, it might help to establish that the cancelled order, coupled with the bank borrowings, forced Pierre to sell.'

'Leave it with me.'

Peter put down the phone and swore out loud. 'That bloody man lied to me about Pierre's gambling and so did Helene Martin.' He paced up and down for a few minute to try to calm down and then decided to call Juliette.

'I just wanted to let you know that it's pretty clear the sale of the company was not straightforward and Hubert clearly pressurised Pierre into selling, having undermined the company's financial position by borrowing to meet his debts. I'm waiting for a little more information from Richard Anstruther but I thought you'd like to know our suspicions were justified.'

'That's awful considering Dad trusted him.'

'I agree, and it looks as though Helene Martin was also involved as well.'

'In what way?'

'Seemingly she was very friendly with the supermarket buyer who placed the original large order and then cancelled it. The order should never have been accepted in the first place as it was larger than they could fulfil.'

'Peter, this is all terribly sad. I really regret not taking more trouble to keep in touch with Dad at the end, because maybe I could have prevented all this.'

'I don't think there's anything you could've done, as this all happened a couple of years before he died and he probably had no idea he was being defrauded.'

'So what can we do about it now?'

'Well, I'm waiting for some more information from Richard Anstruther and, depending on what I hear, I'm planning to go back to Nice to get to the bottom of all this.'

'Would you like me to come with you?'

'You're very welcome, but I'm more than happy to deal with it myself if you're comfortable leaving me to handle it.'

'Of course I am. When are you planning to go?'

'Depending on what I hear from Richard, possibly the day after tomorrow.'

'Maybe you'd let me know where you're staying, as I might try to fly down myself. I'd really like to confront Hubert and hear what he has to say.'

'As soon as I've finalised my plans, I'll let you know.'

'Thank you so much, Peter, I really am most grateful.'

Peter checked on flights and also the availability of rooms at the Westminster in Nice. He decided to wait to hear from Richard before booking but, in the meantime, called his accountant to ask him about the legal position relating to loans by companies to directors. Having established the basis on which they may be permissible, he made his way to Queen's Club for a game of Real Tennis and lunch in order to unwind.

Later in the afternoon, Richard called him again.

'I've now managed to get to the bottom of that supermarket order. As you suspected, Helene Martin was behind it. She encouraged her friend to place an order which was significantly larger than the previous year, despite being aware there could be problems with the crop, which had been affected by the poor spring weather.'

'How did you discover this?'

'From one of the staff at the vineyard – it's amazing what a few drinks and a little cash can do if someone is posing as a journalist wanting information for a story about the company's change in ownership. Apparently, Pierre was not around much at this time and, when the order came in, Hubert was confronted by a couple of the senior staff who told him they couldn't possibly fulfil it. Hubert became quite belligerent and told them to concentrate on production and leave him to worry about running the company. About a month later, they talked to him again and pointed out that production would be well down on the previous year and they wouldn't be able to meet all their customers' orders. He apparently said he'd sort out the problem and the next thing they heard was that the supermarket order had been cancelled.

'This now left them with surplus stock which had to be sold off cheaply and led to major financial problems that were made even worse by its heavy bank borrowings. By the way, there also seems to have been a problem about the use of an EU Development Grant. Our contact's source believes that while all this was going on Hubert had been talking to a couple of wealthy backers who'd indicated they were prepared to help him fund the purchase of the vineyard if he could get it cheaply. Not long after this, the staff were told that Hubert and some external investors had bought the company and Pierre was no longer involved. Hubert claimed Pierre was suffering from the after effects of a minor stroke and also had some early symptoms of Alzheimer's.'

'So now we know how Hubert managed to get the vineyard and the property so cheaply.'

'Absolutely – not surprisingly, the bank had been very concerned about the company's financial position and had refused to renew their loan arrangement until more money was injected and Hubert had repaid his own loan. The new investors provided additional funds and, following the recapitalisation, Hubert significantly increased his personal stake in the business. He also acquired the villa at less than the current market value.'

'Do we have any information about the investors?'

'Yes, one of them was a good friend of Helene Martin, the other owned a much smaller vineyard near Carros. I imagine they may be planning an amalgamation of the businesses at a later stage.'

'So Helene Martin's fingerprints are all over this deal as well as Hubert's. I wonder what she got out of it?'

'I suspect she's been well looked after by Hubert since she set up the supermarket order and then tipped them off about supply problems which led to it being cancelled.'

'I still don't understand why it had such a drastic impact on the business.'

'Simply because they'd stopped taking other orders so, when the supermarket cancelled, they were left with a massive hole with not enough time to fill it.'

'Richard, I'm going to fly to Nice tomorrow to confront Helene Martin about this – can you email the report you've just summarised so that I have ammunition, should I need it?'

'Of course. By the way, Maître Simon is fully briefed about Juliette, the diamonds and this latest development. He is awaiting instructions on how to proceed.'

'Perhaps I can discuss that with you once I'm in Nice.'

'All right, but let me know if I can do anything more to help.'

Peter booked himself into the Westminster and an early flight to Nice the following morning. He wasn't sure exactly what he expected to accomplish, but he was determined to expose how Pierre had been cheated by two people he thought he could trust. He also felt uncomfortable about what he would say to Suzanne and even wondered whether she knew anything about what had occurred. However, he decided to play that by ear once he was in Nice.

The next morning Peter took a cab to the airport, not being sure how long he'd be away and reluctant to leave his car too long in the car park. As usual, the flight was late leaving, but after a welcome breakfast they were over the Alps and fast approaching the crystalline blue Mediterranean which shimmered in the distance, bathed in the morning sunshine. Once through passport control he picked up a taxi, and ten minutes later was drawing up outside his hotel. He had a corner room with doors to a balcony overlooking the Promenade and the other window looking toward Cap Ferrat. He decided to sit for a while on the balcony in the warm midday sunshine to relax and watch the activity below. A mixture of skaters, elderly women with small dogs, holidaymakers on their way to the beach and a never-ending flow of cars and motorbikes passed beneath him, all enjoying the Mediterranean summer sunshine.

Shortly after an excellent fish soup on the terrace of the hotel, he called Suzanne and arranged to have tea with her in the lounge of the Negresco. Whilst waiting, and over a cup of coffee, he reread the report Richard had emailed to him. Appended to it was a summary of the company's financial performance in the three years preceding its sale, which showed a gradual downturn in revenue and increasing bank borrowings – a far from healthy situation. It was also apparent that Hubert's borrowings had been growing steadily throughout that time. There was also a note from the accountants concerning an EU grant which appeared not to have been used for the purpose for which it was originally intended.

When he had finished reading, Peter took a stroll along the Promenade towards the harbour and stopped briefly to join a crowd watching a group of beautifully tanned girls playing beach volleyball. 'Easy to see why it's become an Olympic sport,' he said to an enthusiastic American tourist who was applauding every point.

'Beats watching cricket,' was the smiling reply.

Walking into the Negresco, he had a sense of time standing still, greeted by the doormen in their elaborate uniforms and cockaded hats. He made his way through the vast central marble hall to the oak panelled lounge where he was joined by Suzanne. He kissed her warmly and immediately caught the lingering fragrance of the perfume she had worn when last they had met.

'Peter, it's so nice to see you again, I hope you're not rushing back to London so soon this time.'

'It rather depends on how things work out in the next few days, but it's good of you to come at such short notice and you're looking fantastic.'

'I do my best and your compliment is appreciated. But tell me, how are you getting on? And have you finally got to the bottom of those mysterious boxes that Maman keeps talking about?'

'Before I tell you about that, shall I order us some tea?'

'Please, if they have Earl Grey that would be perfect.'

Having caught the waiter's eye, Peter told her about locating the packing cases and also mentioned the medals, revolver, postcards, letters and files that he had found. He had earlier decided not to say anything more until he met Helene Martin.

'Tell me, Suzanne, why do you think your mother was so interested in the packing cases?'

'I just don't know, but I believe she was under the impression there might be some jewellery amongst the items he left behind in England.'

'Really, I wonder what gave her that idea.'

'She told me that, when Pierre was ill following his stroke, he was often semi-conscious and he talked in a rambling way about diamonds. As you know, he was beginning to suffer from early stage Alzheimer's and I thought it was all imagined, but Maman became convinced that the cases contained hidden valuables.'

'Nothing so exciting, I'm afraid, but I'd like to have a chat with her about what I did find, as it will hopefully mean the lawyers can finalise everything quite quickly. Is she still living at Quai des Etats-Unis?'

'Yes, it's the flat Pierre found for her.'

'I think I still have her phone number. I haven't seen her for over ten years – is her English as good as it used to be?'

'Of course, she has two very good English friends who she sees regularly. One of them has a flat just along the Promenade and she has lunch with them there most weekends.'

'Would you mind mentioning I'll be giving her a call?'

'Of course not. Is there anything I should tell her in advance?'

'No, simply that I want to talk to her about the packing cases and one or two other loose ends.'

'Do you think the lawyers will then be able to finalise things? She seems to be very much on edge as a result of all the uncertainty.'

'I hope so. It's the main reason for my visit, but I also plan to see Hubert to find out how things are going at the vineyard.'

'I hear that he's had a few difficulties since taking over, but I suppose that's to be expected.'

He looked at his watch.

'Suzanne, would you mind if I slipped back to the hotel, as I have to make a couple of calls before the end of the afternoon. I'd love to see you again – could I give you a call tomorrow to try to arrange dinner?'

'That would be fun, Peter, give me a ring when you're free.'

'I'll look forward to it.'

Back at the Westminster, Peter called Richard Anstruther.

'I just met Helene Martin's daughter, Suzanne. Clearly her mother had some inkling about Pierre's diamonds and believed they may have been concealed in the packing cases in England. That may account for her keenness to try to find the cases and even to hire a private detective to help her do so. Apparently she has been quite edgy recently, which may be as a result of a guilty conscience or else anticipation that the cases might reveal something of value. Either way, I propose to confront her about her involvement with the supermarket deal and the resultant forced sale of the company to Hubert.'

'If you could get her to admit to the part she played in helping Hubert and maybe find out if she and Hubert knew about Pierre's past, we'd have a strong case against Hubert for trying to cheat Juliette out of her inheritance. The bizarre thing is that if she hadn't have been so obsessed by those packing cases and the possibility they contained valuables, you might never have found Delphine or Juliette and certainly wouldn't have come across the diamonds.'

'One of those strange twists of fate you'd normally only find in a novel, Richard! Anyhow, I plan to arrange to see her tomorrow, so it should be an interesting meeting.'

'Keep me posted and let me know if I can do anything more to help.'

'Thanks, I'll be in touch.'

Peter rang Helene Martin and found her reaction to his proposed visit less than enthusiastic. However, a meeting was arranged at her flat the following morning.

'I suspect Suzanne has told her there was nothing of value in the packing cases,' he mused. 'Strictly true, but she's going to get a shock when she finds out about the diamonds in the safe deposit box and Juliette's claim to the estate.'

CHAPTER ELEVEN

AFTER A LATE breakfast, he walked through the old market, which was full of stalls selling flowers, vegetables, fruit, bread, meat, fish, cakes, pastries and a vast range of cheeses. The smell of cheese dominated the air and he wondered whether any from Normandy ever found its way this far south. He paused for a while to look at a statue of a man dressed in nineteenth century clothes which had drawn a small crowd, but quickly moved on when it gave him a slow, knowing wink.

Arriving at Helene Martin's apartment building overlooking the Promenade he pressed the entryphone bell and went into a spacious panelled hall with an old-fashioned open lift whose iron gates reminded him of a 1930s film. He took it to the top floor and found her waiting at the door. After a kiss on both cheeks he followed her into a large, sunbathed sitting room with three sets of double doors leading to a balcony looking out to sea. He took a seat on a large sofa opposite her. She looked very much the part of a well maintained woman in her sixties. Dyed blonde hair, heavy make-up, a smart tailored suit, too much jewellery and a somewhat forced smile.

'It's a pleasure to see you again, Peter. How have you been since we last met?'

'I'm fine and I hope all is well with you?'

'As well as can be expected. I'm not getting any younger and life becomes more difficult as one loses one's looks.'

'But that's not a matter to concern you.'

'Peter, your flattery is on a par with Pierre's, but sadly I am a realist. How have you been getting on in trying to resolve his affairs?'

'Well, I think at last the lawyers will be able to close their files as there appear to be no more loose ends.'

'That's very welcome news.'

'I hope it's welcome, although there are a couple of developments that will almost certainly complicate matters.'

'Really, in what way?'

'Firstly there appear to have been some irregularities in the circumstances leading to the sale of Pierre's company and the villa.'

Peter watched Helene Martin's eyes narrow as she took in what he had said.

'What do you mean by "irregularities"?'

'Simply that the sale was forced on Pierre as a result of a contrived financial crisis.'

Before she could say anything further, Peter rose to his feet and walked to the window.

'This really is the most stunning view, it must be spectacular at sunset.'

'It's wonderful, but I'm sure you haven't come here to talk about my view.'

'No, but I am interested in Hubert. I hadn't realised he was also a gambler.'

'Surely you knew Hubert had a weakness for the tables. He used to play blackjack, roulette and also poker here and also in Monte Carlo.'

'Quite the contrary. When I saw him recently he gave me the impression Pierre was the heavy gambler.'

'He played occasionally. We used to go together to Monte Carlo for dinner and then on to the casino. But with Hubert it was something of an addiction.'

'So did Hubert lose quite a lot of money?'

'I'm afraid so. I believe Pierre tried to encourage him to reduce the frequency of his wagering.'

'And I understand he may have borrowed money from the company to cover his debts.'

'I suppose it's possible.'

'Tell me, weren't you surprised when he asked you to persuade your friend at the Laudel Supermarket Group to place such a large order with the company?'

Peter noticed that Mme Martin's neck was now flushed and she took a moment or two before replying.

'Why are you asking me about all this? I know nothing about the company's business.'

'But you used to lunch with the wine buyer regularly and were able to influence her buying decisions.'

'I saw her quite often but it was purely social.'

'That's not quite true. We have information which establishes quite clearly that on one occasion you pressed her to place a much larger order than previously.'

'Well, I may have mentioned that the wine was expected to be particularly good that year and she would do well to increase her order.'

'But that simply isn't true. The crop that year was a disaster following poor spring weather.'

Peter watched as she lost her composure and reached hurriedly for a cigarette.

'Hubert asked me to push for a large order. I didn't know why, but I assumed that they may have lost other orders and needed this to make up for them.'

'But when it was withdrawn and the company found itself in difficulties, you introduced a potential investor who helped Hubert to acquire it.'

'Hubert told me the business was in trouble. I mentioned that I might know someone who could help.'

'And what did he pay you for this "help"?'

She stubbed out her cigarette and became flustered.

'He offered me a fee if he was able to acquire the company and he said he would also like to purchase the villa. Pierre was not well, having recently recovered from a minor stroke. I needed money to maintain myself.'

'Is that why you were so anxious to find out about the contents of the packing cases I located in England?'

'I thought there might be something of value in them from things Pierre had said.'

'This was when he was ill and his mind may have been rambling?'

'I can't recall, but I got the impression there might be some jewellery hidden in them. He had previously told me I would be receiving part of whatever was left from his estate once everything was settled.'

By now she was looking drained despite the make-up. Peter almost felt sorry for her but he was determined to finish what he had come for.

'I mentioned earlier there were a couple of developments. There were no jewels in the packing cases, mostly letters and a key to a safe deposit with BNP Paribas. I traced the box to a branch in Paris and found it contained some uncut diamonds.'

Helene Martin's eyes and mouth opened in astonishment.

'Are they valuable?'

'I've no idea, but they're being transferred to Maître Simon, who'll have them valued for inheritance tax purposes.'

'But how wonderful. So I was right, after all, to press for the boxes to be located and to get a private detective to start searching for them.'

'Perhaps, although I don't think you'll find it has worked out quite as you'd hoped. Tell me, was Hubert reasonably generous with the fee he paid you in view of the way he's benefitted?'

'He took care of me for my efforts. After all, I had to look out for myself, as Pierre was beginning to decline and I had to consider my own future.'

'But surely if Pierre was ill and you were ultimately going to share in the estate it was better for you that Pierre retained the business and the villa?'

'I wasn't absolutely sure I would inherit anything, and Hubert paid my fee immediately.'

Peter now saw her as a sad, insecure and frightened woman who had been used by Hubert to achieve his objectives. He even felt slightly sorry for her and imagined her anxiety as Pierre's health started to deteriorate. Despite this, he couldn't help feeling bitter about the way she had betrayed him and he wondered whether her actions had also been prompted as a result of knowing Juliette's real identity. However, he now decided not to mention this until he had seen Hubert, in case she warned him beforehand.

'Tell me, how much does Suzanne know about this?'

'Only that I helped Hubert to raise the money to buy the company by introducing him to one of the investors.'

'And do you know how it's currently performing?'

'I'm not really sure, as I see Hubert less frequently.'

'Well, I must be going, as I have other matters to deal with. Thank you for your time.'

'Can you tell me anything more about when the legal formalities will be concluded?'

'I have no specific information but I'm sure Maître Simon will be in touch with you shortly. Au revoir.'

As he walked back to his hotel Peter ran over the conversation in his mind. Helene Martin had clearly been used by Hubert and been ready to put her own self-interest ahead of loyalty to Pierre. He found her behaviour despicable but also realised it was as a result of weakness as much as greed. The only thing that gave him any comfort was the knowledge that Suzanne did not appear to have been a party to the deceit.

When he got back to the Westminster, he sat on the terrace, ordered a beer and called Richard Anstruther.

'I've just talked to Helene Martin. She's confirmed exactly what happened and that Hubert paid her a fee for her efforts. I told her about the diamonds but didn't refer to Juliette, as I don't want her to forewarn Hubert.'

'When are you proposing to confront him about this?'

'I think I'll take a chance and go straight up to the villa. I'm sure Helene Martin will have told him about my visit, but if I ring it gives him the chance to put me off.'

'All the best – I suspect it's going to be an uncomfortable meeting.'

'Well, it will be for Hubert!'

After lunch Peter received a call from Suzanne.

'Peter, Maman seems very upset following your visit. She won't tell me why. What's going on?'

'Unfortunately I can't say more until I've talked to Hubert. I'm going to try to see him this afternoon. Assuming I'm back reasonably early, would you like to meet for dinner this evening?'

'Yes, but can't you tell me anything?'

'Not till I've seen Hubert.'

Peter picked up a hire car and, after cutting through the Nice afternoon traffic, once again found himself on the winding road leading to Carros. So much had happened in the short time that had elapsed since he'd made the journey previously. However, now he was about to greet Hubert not as a friend but as someone who had sacrificed friendship for financial gain. As he drove up through the trees, he wondered why Hubert had allowed his personal financial problems to influence his behaviour in such a ruthless manner. He would soon find out. Arriving at the villa, he rang the intercom at the main gate. After a short pause Hubert answered and the gates swung open to enable him to drive up to the house. 'I can understand Hubert coveting this,' thought Peter, 'but his behaviour has been deplorable.'

'Well, this is a surprise,' said Hubert. 'What brings you here?'

'I suspect you probably know already.'

'I'm afraid not – why should I?'

They walked through to the terrace – this time Peter declined a drink.

'I'll get right to the point, Hubert, although I'm sure Helene Martin has already warned you of the reason for my visit. Put bluntly, I know that as a result of personal debt and greed, you contrived a situation that forced Pierre to sell you the vineyard and the villa. I also have information about how you managed, with Helene Martin's help, to exacerbate the financial problems which enabled you and your co-investors to acquire the business and the house for much less than they were worth. But, perhaps more important, I know why you took this course of action to defraud Pierre.'

Hubert had been listening impassively as Peter spoke. Now he reacted.

'That's absolutely outrageous, I very much doubt that you know the true reason I acquired the business and it certainly wasn't fraud.'

'It was because you discovered Juliette Leger was his daughter and you knew she would inherit the estate on his death. You plotted to acquire the business so it wouldn't go to her.'

'What do you mean, Juliette Leger is his daughter?'

'Don't take me for a fool. You found out that Juliette was born as a result of an affair between Pierre and a Resistance leader in Normandy.'

Hubert looked genuinely perplexed.

'Peter I've no idea what you are talking about but it sounds absurd. Pierre never had any children.'

Peter had been watching Hubert closely throughout their exchange and was surprised to find himself considering whether Hubert might be telling the truth.

'Let me assure you she is his daughter and I have seen a certificate confirming it. I simply don't believe you didn't know.'

'How could I know? Pierre always introduced her as the daughter of a good friend from the days of his business dealings in Normandy after the war. There was never anything in the manner of their behaviour to suggest otherwise.'

Peter found he was now seriously beginning to wonder whether to believe Hubert, but then he remembered the unanswered letters from Juliette.

'But, Hubert, Juliette wrote to Pierre two or three times in the months before he died and she received no reply.'

'All right, Peter, I now have no alternative but to share confidences Pierre asked me not to reveal to anyone else. After Pierre had a slight stroke about three or four years ago he gradually started to become quite forgetful. We talked about this from time to time as he became more aware of its effects both on him and the business. He could be obstinate but also very charming, and he persuaded me to cover up for him if problems arose as a result of his condition.

'It became more difficult when he started borrowing money from the company without it being properly accounted for. I subsequently found out that when Helene had been away one weekend she had asked Suzanne to spend some time with him and, like an old fool, he had started flirting with her. As you know, he always looked good for his age and he was both sophisticated and charming. To cut a long story short, he started seeing her behind her mother's back and lavished expensive gifts on her. On one occasion a bill for a car arrived at the company and had to be honoured. He was behaving like a lovesick youngster and, although I don't think there was anything more to it than infatuation, he was obviously flattered by her apparent interest. I tried to curb his extravagance but he was treating the business like a piggy bank.

'I realised that, as he gradually became more forgetful and unpredictable, I had to take action, because I'd been obliged to cover up his activities by claiming the missing money had been loaned to me, as he was in no position to repay it, and loans to Pierre wouldn't have looked good in the accounts. There was also a problem with an EU Development Grant that was intended to accelerate the company's expansion but which he used inappropriately. So to cut a long story short, I planned to buy the business to save it from collapse and, as he no longer needed the house, I bought it at slightly less than the market price to reimburse me for the loans he'd incurred but I'd been obliged to cover.

'The scheme wasn't particularly sophisticated but it worked. Nobody realised the problems he'd caused and he was able to stay on at the lodge. Sadly, during the last year of his life, he went downhill, but he insisted on having Suzanne look after his personal affairs. She used to come up to the lodge twice a week and she seemed to cheer him up, but I never knew exactly what she was doing as I was at the vineyard. Meanwhile Helene continued seeing him, although much less frequently – I think she probably only saw him to make sure the bills for her flat were paid by his bank.'

'But surely if this was happening Helene would have known.'

'I'm not sure whether she suspected and turned a blind eye, or whether she knew and didn't care any longer. She and Suzanne were never very close. Either way, her influence had totally diminished, whilst Suzanne appeared to be able to twist Pierre round her finger. But I'm astonished by what you say about Juliette. On the few occasions I met them together he behaved to her like a friend – nothing ever suggested a closer relationship.'

'Well, I can assure you it's true and there are documents to prove it.'

By now Peter was confused. If what Hubert was saying was correct, Pierre's financial problems had been largely self-induced and, although the way Hubert had sought to save the business was unorthodox, it had at least prevented its total collapse.

'When you created the financial crisis with the cancelled supermarket order was Pierre not suspicious?'

'I think he could have been, but by then he was becoming very forgetful. I got Helene to persuade him that the sale of the business was the only solution.'

'For which you paid her a fee.'

'For that and the role she played with the supermarket. And additionally for introducing me to a couple of financial backers.'

'I find the whole story very perplexing. I met Juliette in Paris and she told me she didn't hear anything from her father in the year before he died, despite writing. She said she hadn't been in touch so frequently in the last few years but was surprised not to get replies to her letters. She also tried calling but there were problems with the phone.'

'I think that was at Suzanne's instigation. She claimed he was beginning to become a nuisance, calling her frequently very late at night and asking her to come to see him. There wasn't really a need for a phone. The housekeeper here looked after his meals and laundry and I popped in to see him every day. Helene came up once a week and Suzanne was here two or three times a week.'

'Did you say Suzanne looked after his personal affairs?'

'Yes, there wasn't a lot to do once he moved into the lodge, but she took care of correspondence and anything else that needed to be dealt with as I was at the vineyard most of the day.'

'What did he do with his time?'

'He used to potter in the garden and he would listen to music. He watched a lot of quiz programmes – I can't imagine why – and had lunch occasionally with a couple of elderly business friends. He was reasonably content, especially when Suzanne appeared, invariably with a new dress, bag or piece of jewellery. I think he'd arranged for her to have a credit card and she kept busy using it. Towards the end he deteriorated quite fast and really showed signs of Alzheimer's, so we had to organise a nurse to be with him. At that stage Suzanne was very good and spent a lot of time here herself.'

'Who took care of the funeral arrangements?'

'Suzanne. It was a low-key affair at the church here in Carros. There were about a dozen people altogether – Helene, Suzanne and me, Maître Simon, the housekeeper, two or three of his old friends from Nice, the manager of the vineyard and his nurse.'

'Do you know why I wasn't notified about his death until after the funeral, and then by Maître Simon?'

'Suzanne dealt with everything, Peter, I don't know who she asked or, indeed, who may have been invited but was unable to attend.'

'I must say I find it amazing that Juliette was not contacted either.'

'Peter, you must accept that what you have just told me about Juliette being Pierre's daughter comes as a complete surprise, just as it must have been to you. I don't know why Suzanne failed to notify her – perhaps she didn't think they were especially close. After all, Pierre was not very lucid towards the end and had lost touch with many of his past acquaintances.'

Peter found himself bewildered by Hubert's account of events and was torn between accepting his story and still suspecting him of acting improperly. He was also shocked by the revelations about Suzanne's behaviour.

'Tell me, Hubert, is there anyone who can corroborate what you have told me about the company's financial problems?'

'Of course, our lawyers and accountants would be able to confirm what I have told you, although I suspect they would only talk to Maître Simon.'

'Very well. I apologise if this has been uncomfortable for you, but you must see that the whole business appears to be very curious. Please let me have the contact details for your two advisers and the matter can then be forgotten.'

Peter got up to leave and, as he did so, Hubert rose and put an arm round his shoulder.

'Believe me, Peter, I had great regard for your uncle. We've been business colleagues for many years and from time to time in the past may have had differences of opinion over the occasional deal, but Pierre was a good friend and I did the best I could at the end, in very difficult circumstances. I haven't profited personally in any way from the steps I took. In fact the company's reputation has been suffering quite badly recently following the problems that stemmed from Pierre's cavalier use of its money and also a loss of orders. With the benefit of hindsight there might have been a better way to solve the problem, but I felt that only by shocking Pierre would he accept he had no alternative but to sell. Sadly I fear that the course of action I took may have come too late. I hope you now understand what happened and why I acted as I did. More important, I'd like to feel that next time we meet it'll be in more friendly circumstances.'

'I hope so too.'

Once he was away from the house Peter called Richard Anstruther and explained what had happened. He asked him to contact Maître Simon and get him to check Hubert's story with the company's two advisers.

'What are your plans now?' said Richard.

'I have to see Suzanne, but before doing so I must talk to Juliette and would also like to hear whether Maître Simon can corroborate Hubert's explanation.'

'I will get on to it right away.'

Back in Nice he called Juliette.

'I meant to call you earlier but things have moved rather faster than I expected. I have answers to some of our concerns but I need to hear from Richard Anstruther before I can be really confident we know the full story. I promise to call you as soon as the situation is clearer. In the meantime, have you given any more thought to what you will do with the diamonds?'

'Peter, I'm happy to wait until you're ready. As to the diamonds, I have some ideas but let's talk when you have resolved the situation down there.'

'That sounds fine to me, I hope to be able to call tomorrow.'

He sat on the terrace at the hotel nursing a cold beer. It was now nearly 5.30 and he didn't want to see Suzanne until he'd heard from Richard. He thought it was unlikely there'd be news before the morning, so he had another beer and then called her.

'I'm just back from my meeting with Hubert – would you mind very much if we changed the arrangement and met for lunch tomorrow?'

'Oh, Peter, I was looking forward to seeing you and hoping you'd tell me what's going on. Maman is refusing to talk to me but seems very upset following your meeting. Don't you even have time for a drink?'

'I'm feeling rather tired and I still have things to do – I'd prefer to make it tomorrow, if that's all right.'

'Of course, I'll call you in the morning to arrange when and where to meet.'

Peter felt relieved that the meeting with Suzanne had been postponed, as he was in no mood for further emotional conversations. Deciding to have a local fish speciality for dinner, he headed to the old town and was soon sitting at an outside table overlooking the market. He ordered Bouillabaisse and, whilst he waited, he sampled a local white wine that the waiter recommended. He had just started to eat when his mobile rang – it was Richard.

'I hope it's not too late as you're an hour ahead, but I thought you might like to know that Maître Simon had a quick word with the lawyer whose name you gave me. He was a bit evasive at first, but then confirmed that Pierre had apparently got himself into some sort of trouble with an EU grant and he'd also made some largish unauthorised cash drawings. It was all smoothed over by Hubert, who claimed the loans were his. It seems to confirm Hubert is speaking the truth and that Pierre's failing memory was putting the business at serious risk.'

'Thanks, Richard. I'm just having supper but that's something of a relief. I was finding it very depressing to think that, at the end of his life, Pierre was surrounded by a bunch of parasites all trying to take advantage of him. I'm sure Juliette will be pleased to hear the news as well.'

Peter finished his meal and strolled back along the Promenade to the hotel. A full moon was just appearing on the horizon and the waves shimmered gently in its glow. Stopping for a while, he watched as it rose higher and the sea took on an eerie appearance as if the light came from underwater. He found himself thinking of the night Pierre had parachuted into France and imagined the plane searching for the drop zone guided to its target by lights flickering in the darkness below. Resuming his walk, he reflected on the news that Hubert appeared to have acted in the best interests of the business. He found this reassuring, although the manner in which Hubert had contrived its rescue still made him feel uncomfortable. More worrying was the news that it was still in difficulty.

After breakfast the next morning he called Suzanne and proposed lunch at La Rotonde in the Negresco. He thought she sounded tense, but he avoided conversation by saying he was on his way to a meeting. Shortly afterwards, Richard Anstruther called again.

'Maître Simon has spoken to the accountants. They confirm that the company was in a mess and they'd spoken to Hubert about a number of problems long before he acquired it. They were concerned about the apparent misuse of the EU Development Grant and also the level of petty cash drawings made by Pierre. Apparently they were proposing to put a qualification on the auditor's report which would not have been well received by the bank. Hubert agreed to assume responsibility for the missing monies and to characterise them as personal loans. This satisfied the auditors, but they were concerned about Pierre's continued involvement and they urged that he should leave the board. It seems that Hubert's action, albeit clumsy, was well intentioned and partially influenced by their advice as, without an apparent crisis, Pierre would never have let go and the business would have gone under. They also told Maître Simon that, although Hubert is doing his best, the business is still losing money, is undercapitalised and would benefit from a more dynamic Sales Director.'

'That's fairly depressing news, but it's clear Hubert's actions were well intentioned.'

'I think so. Obviously the ploy to precipitate the crisis made Pierre accept the inevitable, but the future doesn't look great. Unless their fortunes improve considerably it looks as though the company may not survive.'

Peter sat on his balcony reading until it was time to meet Suzanne for lunch. He had always liked La Rotonde's quirky atmosphere, with its circular shape and the roundabout feature with the fairground horses that entertained small visitors as they pranced up and down when the organ played. Once he was seated at a booth on the side, he ordered a Kir and was glancing at the menu when Suzanne arrived.

'Hello, Peter, what are you drinking?'

'A Kir, would you like one?'

'Yes, please.'

When the wine came she drank hurriedly and seemed tense. He decided to get to the point immediately.

'Have you spoken to your mother since I saw her yesterday?'

'Yes, briefly. She was very tight-lipped and said you'd been rather unpleasant about the circumstances surrounding the sale of the vineyard. She refused to say anything more.'

'Suzanne, I need to understand what happened between you and Pierre about two or three years ago, once he began to become forgetful and the business started to incur financial problems.'

'What do you mean?' she said defensively.

'Simply that I know he started lavishing gifts on you and also bought you a car using the company's money.'

'He was fond of me and was a very generous person.'

'But then he gave you a credit card which you used heavily and he charged to the company.'

'Well that was to cover my expenses and to express his appreciation for my help.'

'What exactly were you doing for him?'

She started to shift uncomfortably and hurriedly swallowed the rest of her wine. Peter signalled the waiter to bring her another glass.

'I kept him company. We sat in the garden and talked. I looked after his personal correspondence and liaised with the housekeeper about his meals. I even joined him sometimes when he had his boring old friends to lunch. I liked him, he was charming and he was attracted to me. I know he was in his seventies but, although his memory was fading, he always seemed happy when he saw me.'

'Wasn't this more a case of you taking advantage of a frail elderly man?'

'Not at all, it was he who made overtures to me one weekend when Maman asked me to spend time with him.'

'So you decided to take advantage of his attraction to you?'

'I admit I responded a little, he was still a good-looking man for his age and, as I said, was very charming, but there was never more than a flirtation between us.'

Peter decided to confront her about Juliette's letters.

'Whilst you were helping him Juliette Leger wrote a couple of times but she received no reply. What happened to her letters?'

'I don't remember, but I do recall seeing them. I think he kept all her letters in a box. He wasn't able to write letters towards the end. I simply dealt with business correspondence with his bank, insurance matters, personal bills and so on.'

'So you didn't think letters from his daughter were important?'

'What?'

'Juliette Leger was his daughter.'

'Are you pulling my leg?'

'No, Juliette was born as a result of a wartime relationship when he was with the Free French. She was born at the end of the war – her mother still lives in Normandy.'

'Are you serious? Pierre never said anything about having a daughter. I only met her once and was under the impression she was the daughter of one of his friends.'

Once again Peter found himself totally perplexed by Pierre's behaviour, and that he had obviously said nothing about his relationship to Juliette, even at the end of his life.

'But surely you realised the letters were from his daughter?'

'Why should I? I seem to remember she addressed him as "Cher P" and not as "Cher Papa", and signed her letters "Tres affectueusement".'

'And he never mentioned she was his daughter.'

'Peter, I've already said so. To be quite blunt, he was more like a child during the last year of his life. We even played games like hide and seek in the grounds and he got very excited when he caught me and gave me a kiss. It was all very chaste.'

'But you were not above accepting gifts from a frail, elderly man?'

'I'm not especially proud of what I did, but I made him happy and it wasn't very easy, as he really was rather pathetic right at the end. Maman saw him less and less and he was very lonely. For me it was like a job and I could easily pop in when I wasn't showing flats or houses to potential buyers.'

'And when he died, why weren't Juliette and I asked to the funeral?'

'As you probably know, he was a very private man and never liked fuss. He was suffering quite badly with Alzheimer's at the end, so it was impossible to discuss anything with him. Hubert asked me to take care of the funeral, as he had various problems at the vineyard. Perhaps I should have thought of contacting you but, as far as I was aware, you hadn't been in touch for many years and I didn't have an address for you. It wouldn't have crossed my mind to ask Juliette, as I hardly knew her.'

Peter fell silent and was only interrupted by a waiter enquiring whether they would like to order.

'I'd like a fillet steak with a salad,' said Suzanne.

'I'll have the same with the pommes frites.'

'And to drink?'

'Just some water.'

As the waiter disappeared, the fairground music started and the merry-go-round horses briefly pranced up and down their poles to the obvious delight of many of the restaurant's young customers.

'Peter, do you mind if I ask how long you've known Juliette Leger was Pierre's daughter and why you haven't mentioned it before?'

'I only found out from papers Pierre left in some packing cases in England.'

'Not the boxes Maman has been insisting contained valuables?'

'Yes.'

'Well, were there any valuables?'

Peter was once again reluctant to disclose more than was necessary.

'No, nothing of value. Files, letters, some medals, a revolver and some photos.'

He told her briefly of his search, culminating firstly in meeting Delphine and subsequently Juliette.

'What an extraordinary story. So you didn't know anything about Juliette either until a week or two ago?'

'No, I guess we've all been kept in the dark.'

'But isn't it sad that because of this dreadful illness he died without her being here.'

'I think it's tragic, but he chose to live in denial all his life and he paid the inevitable price.'

'What's going to happen to his estate now, because Juliette will become the principal beneficiary?'

'I really don't know. I guess that's for Maître Simon to sort out. In the meantime, I'll have to apologise to your mother for suggesting that she and Hubert conspired to defraud Pierre.'

'Over the sale of the vineyard and the house?'

'Yes, I thought Hubert had been dishonest and I now realise he was trying to deal with a difficult situation the best way he could.'

'I don't know exactly what's happening with the business but I rather get the impression from Maman that ever since Hubert took over it's been going downhill. He recently asked her if she knew of any other potential investors because the bank is reluctant to lend any more and he already has a mortgage on the house.'

'I hadn't appreciated it was that bad, although the lawyer in London told me things weren't going particularly well. I suspect it needs additional money and some more dynamic management – it's a great shame that it's had so many problems.'

'Peter, I must say I feel really uncomfortable about how you may be interpreting the time I spent with Pierre. I didn't take advantage of him, although I admit I was very happy to be indulged. It wasn't easy and I felt I had earned what he gave me.'

'I can understand how it happened, Suzanne, and the whole situation was bizarre – I guess in the end Pierre reaped what he sewed!'

'So have you finished what you set out to achieve?'

'I think so. I have to make a few more calls and will probably be here for another couple of days.'

'Any chance of getting together again before you go?'

'Of course, and I promise to be less tense next time!'

CHAPTER TWELVE

PETER WALKED QUICKLY back to his hotel. He had an idea he wanted to discuss with Juliette, but before doing so he quickly briefed her about his various discussions, particularly the reason why she had not been notified of her father's death.

'Juliette, I need to find out more about the company's current situation from Richard Anstruther and the accountants but, subject to the scale of the problem, I wondered whether you might be prepared to consider using some of the money you'll inherit to help resuscitate it.'

'Quite apart from the money, do you think it would be a wise move?'

'It's difficult to say, but I believe the root of its problems go right back to the time Pierre's health started to deteriorate and he became careless with its funds. I don't think Hubert put enough cash into the business when he acquired it and there's obviously a pressing need for some additional management and better marketing. I just thought you might like to think about it.'

'I don't have much idea what I'm going to inherit, Peter, but I'll give it some thought. In the meantime, do you know if the diamonds have yet been transferred to Maître Simon?'

'No, but I'll check and call you back.'

Next he called Richard Anstruther and brought him up to date about his conversation with Suzanne.

'What a mess,' said Richard. 'Pierre seems to have created chaos around him throughout his life.'

'Mostly caused by his penchant for female company! Tell me, is there any more news about the diamonds?'

'There is, and I wonder if you'd like to guess their value?'

'I've no idea – maybe £100,000?'

'Would you believe, closer to one and a half million euros!'

'You're not serious.'

'I certainly am. Apparently Maître Simon had them transferred to Nice and then asked Van Cleef & Arpels in Cannes to take a look in case they were interested before going to auction. They've asked for an option on three of the stones which they value at around one million euros.'

'Well that means Juliette will be very wealthy even after tax is paid on the estate.'

'Absolutely. I have a feeling Maître Simon is giving her the good news today, which means everything is pretty well completed as far as we lawyers are concerned – apart from submitting our bill!'

'I'm very pleased to hear it, Richard, but there's one thing I'd be grateful if you could look into. It's clear the company needs more capital. Would you mind asking the accountants how much they think is required to get it back into good shape?'

'Why, what's on your mind?'

'I thought Juliette might consider taking back control of the business that should have been part of her heritage had things been different.'

'An interesting idea, Peter, leave it with me.'

Peter now called Hubert.

'Hubert, I've been thinking about my conversation with you, and in particular about the company's current difficulties. How much extra capital would make a difference?'

'Well there are three problems. One of the external shareholders wants to get out. We need additional capital for equipment and there's also a requirement for more working capital, as the bank won't extend our facilities.'

'So what are we talking about?'

'I estimate about 500,000 euros.'

'And would that be sufficient to turn the business round?'

'Yes, although we could use a good marketing man and some additional management.'

'I have a couple of ideas Hubert. Let me get back to you.'

Peter sat on his balcony pondering the conversation with Hubert and wondering whether it was right to encourage Juliette to consider an investment in the business. Perhaps it was irrational to suggest such a scheme but, equally, it had been a good business before Pierre became ill and he felt sure it could be successful again. His phone rang and he saw it was Richard's number.

'The accountants believe the company needs around 300,000 to 400,000 euros for additional working capital. Apparently the bank won't play ball, as the business has been going gradually downhill since Hubert took over. Not particularly because of him, more the legacy of Pierre's mismanagement. They reckon that, with some modern equipment and extra marketing effort, the business has very good potential.'

'Richard, thanks for that, I'm going to give it a little more thought, then I'll talk to Juliette.'

Sitting in the sun, taking in the sights and sounds of the Promenade, Peter realised how much he loved the south of France, and he found himself wishing he could spend more time in Nice. Perhaps he should consider buying a small apartment rather than staying at expensive hotels.

His musings were interrupted by an excited call from Juliette.

'Peter, I've just had a call from Maître Simon. You'll never believe how much he thinks the diamonds may be worth.'

'I can't imagine.'

'He says they could fetch one and a half million euros – possibly more.'

'Juliette, that's incredible.'

'I know, and I find it difficult to believe. I'm so grateful to you for tracing me and also for being so tenacious in locating the safe deposit.'

'Nonsense, I'm sure the bank would have found some way of locating you eventually.'

'I've decided to fly down to Nice, as there are a couple of things I'd like to discuss with you and I also want to meet Maître Simon. Can you reserve me a room where you're staying?'

'Certainly, when will you be here?'

'I have a flight at 7.20 this evening. Can we meet for breakfast at eight o'clock tomorrow morning?'

'I look forward to it.'

Peter ordered from room service and spent the evening rereading the report on the company and making notes. He went for a nightcap at one of the bars on the Promenade and noticed that, if anything, there appeared to be more people out strolling than during the daytime. It was a warm, still evening and music wafted up from the various beach bars which were full of late evening diners, some of whom were dancing on a floor not much larger than a generous sized beach towel. When he got back to the hotel, he checked that Juliette had booked in and reserved a quiet table for breakfast.

He was already at the table when Juliette arrived the next morning.

'Hello, Peter, how are you?'

'Absolutely fine, did you sleep well?'

'After I got used to the traffic. I'm not keen on air conditioning and left the balcony door ajar, which was probably a mistake. Shall we order?'

'How do you feel about coffee and croissants?'

'Perfect, but with some fresh orange juice, please.'

Peter ordered whilst Juliette produced a notepad from her bag.

'I've thought more about your proposal that I should put money into the business. Do you have any idea how much would be required?'

Peter ran through the figures he had been given by Hubert and the accountants. He also emphasised the need for additional marketing resources and mentioned the external investor who wanted to sell his shares.

'So, to provide sufficient funds to recapitalise the company and buy out the investor would require around 500,000 euros?'

'I think that would give it a strong balance sheet which would mean that, if additional funds were required from time to time in future, you could resort to bank borrowing.'

'If I invested 500,000 euros would that give me control?'

'I think you're in a strong position to demand it in view of the poor financial situation.'

'So what do you think I should do?'

'Well, I've also been thinking about it. If you'd like me to invest I thought I might become a shareholder as well.'

'Peter, that's fantastic and makes me feel much more confident. What would be the next step?'

'I think I should talk the accountants and establish what they consider to be its current value and then we could make an offer.'

'That would be great. But there's just one other thing I wanted to mention. I'd like you to choose one of the diamonds as a present with my thanks for everything you've done for me.'

'That's not necessary.'

'I would like you to have it and I know Dad would approve.'

'Are you really sure?'

'Yes, I don't want you to end up with a smaller legacy, having taken so much trouble to unravel Dad's past. Hopefully that'll mean you'll feel all your efforts were worthwhile.'

'Juliette, I know they were, but thank you for your generosity. I'll get on to the accountants right away.'

A couple of days later, Peter and Juliette met Hubert at Maître Simon's office to finalise her purchase of 45% of the company and to enable Peter to acquire the 10% stake held by the external investor. Hubert was genuinely delighted at the prospect of an improvement in the company's fortunes and proposed a toast with a bottle of the Vaillant 2001 rosé.

'To the future of the Vaillant label and its success in the hands of the new family shareholders!'

'I look forward to seeing the wine in my favourite restaurant in Paris before too long,' said Juliette.

'With a good marketing plan, I think we should also be aiming for the UK market within the next couple of years,' countered Peter.

When he was back at the hotel Peter made three more calls.

'Delphine, I have a great deal to tell you, but not on the phone. I'm planning to be in Normandy within the next few weeks – may I pop in to see you again and also sample your delicious apple pie?'

His next call was to Richard Anstruther.

'Richard, job done. I think you should start looking for a new work of art!'

Finally he called Suzanne.

'I'm planning to spend more time in Nice from now on and, despite our last encounter, I'd like to feel we'll see more of each in future. Would you care to join me for lunch tomorrow at the Ephrussi Villa in Cap Ferrat, I've a lot to talk to you about!'

www.ingramcontent.com/pod-product-compliance
Lightning Source LLC
Chambersburg PA
CBHW051142020726
47501CB00005B/1630